MYSTERY AT SMOKEY MOUNTAIN

YWAM Publishing is the publishing ministry of Youth With A Mission. Youth With A Mission (YWAM) is an international missionary organization of Christians from many denominations dedicated to presenting Jesus Christ to this generation. To this end, YWAM has focused its efforts in three main areas: 1) Training and equipping believers for their part in fulfilling the Great Commission (Matthew 28:19). 2) Personal evangelism. 3) Mercy ministry (medical and relief work).
For a free catalog of books and materials write or call:
YWAM Publishing
P.O. Box 55787, Seattle, WA 98155
(206)771-1153 or (800) 922-2143

Mystery at Smokey Mountain

Published by Youth With A Mission Publishing
P.O. Box 55787
Seattle, WA 98155

ISBN 0-927545-65-9

Printed in the United States of America.

To all the
King's Kids of
Youth With A Mission
and to all those
who give their lives to serve
kids of any age.

Other

REEL KIDS
Adventures

The Missing Video
Mystery at Smokey Mountain
The Stolen Necklace
The Mysterious Case
The Amazon Stranger
The Dangerous Voyage
The Lost Diary
The Forbidden Road

Acknowledgments

My visit to Manila's Tondo area was a heartbreaking experience. Even more shocking was learning that 40,000 kids die every day worldwide.

My visit was made easier as I saw some of God's most precious servants laying down their lives to touch hurting humanity. Thank God for all the "Mother Teresas" in the world.

I'll never forget the Anderson family. They had sold everything to follow Jesus and were working daily to make life easier for the poor on the garbage dump in Manila. I saw something special in their eyes. Special thanks to Dave and Mary and their kids for their sacrifice and for key insights in helping me with this book. Their personal experience was invaluable.

I want to thank my wife, Debbie, who ministers to little kids daily. I also thank God for two wonderful gifts—my daughters, Jamie and Katie. I trust they will give their lives to make an impact on a hurting world.

Thanks to David Cunningham of David and David Productions in Hermosa Beach, California. His commitment to help me understand video production is very helpful.

Thanks to all the team at YWAM Publishing, and especially to Pam Warren. They are so committed to presenting truth to a confused world.

And then there's my editor, Shirley Sells. Without her, this book would be incomplete. Editors come along at just the right time to check details and put in the finishing touches. Thanks, Shirley, for your gift.

And thanks to all my friends on staff with Youth With A Mission, Los Angeles. It's fun to work with a dedicated team who give their lives to train kids for their destiny.

I trust that this book will inspire hundreds of kids to travel to the hurting places of the world and share the compassion of Jesus.

Table of Contents

Chapter 1

Frustrated

We've been robbed!"

Jeff Caldwell circled the bags next to the conveyer belt and counted them for the third time. No matter how many times he counted, he always came up one short.

"What's wrong?" K.J. asked nonchalantly as he wandered up, slurping a Coke.

"K.J. Baxter, I can't believe you! You're 14 years old and you're in charge of our equipment. You go off and leave it alone right in the middle of Manila International Airport. Well, guess what! Our camera bag's gone."

Jeff wiped the sweat off his forehead, then dried his hand on his shirt. He pushed a damp blond curl away from his face. He was sweating so heavily that his turquoise shirt and dark jeans looked as if they had been glued to his body. When he turned to face K.J., anger had replaced fatigue in his clear blue eyes.

Although he was only 5'9", a mere three inches taller than K.J., and only a year older, now he seemed to tower over him like a parent disciplining a naughty child. It was all Jeff could do to keep from grabbing K.J. by the shoulders and giving him a good shake.

"Gee, I was only gone a minute. I just went to get something to drink." K.J. returned Jeff's glare with dark, innocent eyes and batted lashes long enough to fill many a girl with envy.

K.J. set his Coke on the floor and pulled at an imaginary loose thread on his T-shirt. He was wearing his new one with the L.A. Dodgers logo. He busied himself in examining his well-worn tennis shoes while he took a plastic comb out of his jeans pocket and nervously pulled it through his thick, dark hair. Jeff had learned to accept this sign of K.J.'s frustration, but right now, it annoyed him to no end.

"Maybe Mindy or Rebecca picked it up," K.J. said hopefully.

Jeff looked around for his sister, Mindy, two years his junior, and spotted her curled on a bench across the waiting room. She was sleeping like a little angel with long legs tucked up neatly under her chest. Her head was resting on the arm of Rebecca, who also had her eyes closed and was breathing rhythmically and heavily. The bag was nowhere in sight.

It was easy to understand why they were so tired. Everyone was exhausted from last-minute packing, a long flight from Los Angeles, and a six-hour delay in Honolulu.

Warren Russell walked up and Jeff greeted him with, "Well, Warren, our camera bag's been stolen." He shot a blistering look in K.J.'s direction. "K.J. left it sitting here and went off to get something to drink."

"Oh, no!" Warren said, and stroked his chin. "Are you sure? Our return tickets and Rebecca's passport were in there." He shook his head.

Warren was an inch taller than Jeff and had his same medium build. He wore his sandy brown hair cropped short enough to pass military inspection. His soft brown eyes were friendly and warm. He was dressed in beige khaki slacks, a blue and green cotton short-sleeved shirt with a geometric design, and brown loafers without socks. Even though he was in his early 30s, he looked young enough to be mistaken for one of his students. Adding to the confusion, the group called him by his first name when they were away from school—with his permission, of course.

Warren headed Baldwin Heights High School's communications department. He chaperoned all the trips of the Reel Kids Club, an organization he had formed to take Christian students on outreach trips to other countries. The club produced videos to show church youth groups, hoping to inspire the churches to send out teams of their own. They met off campus, but were allowed to use school equipment.

Jeff Caldwell had been the first student to join the club. He was excited by the opportunity to share his faith and develop communications skills at the same time because both of his parents worked in the field. His father was a TV anchorman for a large Los Angeles station, and his mother was a news correspondent. Jeff's ambition was to set up a video production company when he got out of college.

Jeff was in charge of the team's finances; K.J., short for Kyle James, was its crackerjack cameraman; and Mindy was its ace reporter. Mindy also did the research for their trips because she loved to ask questions and always took her laptop computer with her everywhere she went. Rebecca Estrella, newest member of the team, had been recruited especially for this trip since she had grown up in the Philippines. They were to stay at her uncle's house.

While Warren went to report the theft, Jeff walked outside in an attempt to cool off physically and emotionally. The heat was almost unbearable, and the dust mingled with exhaust fumes set him off in a fit of coughing.

Jeff didn't want to deal with all the questions racing around in his mind: Why was K.J. always so careless? Who would want their camera bag? And how could they make a video without any equipment? Also, how would Rebecca get back into the United States without a passport?

As his frustration grew, he sat down on a brick planter and watched Mindy walk toward him. All 5′2″ of her seemed mustered to console him. Her pale yellow ponytail matched her shirt and shorts and bounced emphatically with every step. Her intense brown eyes were the color of the rims around her glasses. She broke into a wide grin, exposing a network of silvery braces.

"You're really upset, aren't you?" she asked, twirling her ponytail around two fingers. She punched him playfully on the arm. "Lighten up, big brother. It'll be all right."

He snapped back, "Don't you realize the seriousness of this?"

"You take everything too seriously," she said. "What can we do about it?"

"Nothing, I guess," Jeff said. "Just wait for Rebecca's uncle to pick us up. Do we have any choice?"

Just then, as if by magic, a taxi pulled up to the curb a short distance away.

"Look, there he is now," Mindy said excitedly, pointing to a man climbing out of the back seat. He wore a wrinkled cream-colored suit with large padded shoulders and baggy pants. The pants were belted low beneath a round potbelly. Dark, unruly hair protruded from beneath an off-white straw hat. His bushy eyebrows partially hid his eyelids. He mopped at his brow with one hand and held up a sign reading "Reel Kids Club" with the other.

Jeff and Mindy hurried to meet him.

"You must be Fernando Domingo," Jeff said, sticking out his hand. "I'm Jeff Caldwell with the Reel Kids, and this is my sister, Mindy."

"Pleased to meet you. Where's my niece?"

"She's inside with the others. We've had a small crisis. One of our bags was stolen and our leader is talking to the airport police right now.

"Also, I hate to tell you this, but Rebecca's passport was in the bag, so were our return tickets and all our video equipment."

Jeff scrutinized this man who was so crucial to their mission. Not only was he their host, but he was part of the Presidential Commission for the Urban Poor. Mr. Domingo's forehead creased and his eyebrows drew closer together. His dark brown eyes were solemn and he appeared to be deep in thought.

"That's bad news," he finally said. "The passport could be a big problem. You'll have to be very careful while you're here," he warned them. "We have a lot of theft because of our economy."

While he was talking, Rebecca ran up with the others close behind. She was the same age as K.J. and two inches taller than Mindy. She had dark eyes and straight black hair which was parted in the center and fell almost to her waist. Her creamy almond skin was striking against her bright blue and red flowered dress. She greeted her uncle with a big hug.

Warren put a hand on her shoulder and promised, "I'll go to the American Embassy with you tomorrow and help you get another passport. We'll need some new return tickets, too." Then he told everyone about his talk with the police. He said that the police thought the thief was someone who worked at the airport or had some kind of important connections since he must have escaped through a security door. Otherwise, he'd have had to produce a luggage tag to pass through customs.

Rebecca's uncle also offered to help with the passport. He suggested that since it was Sunday and they couldn't do anything about it until the next day, they should go to his house and rest up. They could start to work on it the next day. "We'll need two taxis," he said as he waved toward the taxi line. "Mr. Russell and I can take the luggage in one, and the rest of you can ride in the other."

"Ours better be air-conditioned," K.J. whispered to Mindy and Rebecca. "You-Know-Who is still pretty steamed up."

Once seated in the taxi, Jeff began to relax. He thought about the reason they were there. "It seems like a long way to go for a garbage dump," he had said when Warren first told him about the trip to the Philippines, even though he normally jumped at any excuse to travel. "An awfully long way."

But the more Warren explained it, the more excited everyone had become until finally they could hardly wait to get there. They were on a mission of love to one of the poorest areas in the world.

Their plan was to produce a video which would raise enough money to purchase water lines for Smokey Mountain, a garbage dump created from an old landfill reclaimed from the bay in the Tondo district of Manila. About 20,000 people made their home on this one-square-mile dump, and from the best information the group could find, an estimated $5,000 was needed for the water project.

As they maneuvered through the dense weekend traffic, Jeff tried to get his mind off their problem. He began looking for some of the old Filipino jeepneys Mindy had told him about. The original ones had been converted from U.S. Army jeeps. They had two benches in the back and although they were designed to hold 12 people, supposedly as many as 20 were often crammed inside. They were painted every color of the rainbow and decorated with tassels, badges, horns, lights, and everything else conceivable.

Mindy said the original jeepneys were a declining species, having given way to more modern expensive Japanese ones, or Southeast Asian utility vehicles which were manufactured locally. According to her guide book, the way to signal when you wanted to get off a jeepney was simply to hiss loudly. They had all tried to outdo each other practicing their hissing.

Mindy nudged Jeff and pointed to a sign over the taxi's rear view mirror: In God We Trust.

Rebecca nodded. "A lot of the people here are raised in church. They believe in God, but they don't know Him in a personal way."

"Are you still upset with me?" K.J. asked Jeff.

Jeff looked him directly in the face. K.J. was the joker in the group—the class clown. He was the one who always got them into jams. Sometimes all he seemed to care about was girls and cars.

"What do you think? You knew better than to leave our things unguarded."

"Well, Mr. Perfect," K.J. snapped back, "maybe you'd like it if I just turned around and went home."

"Quit being such a martyr. Look, this trip is too important to mess up. We've got a chance to help a lot of people if things work out right."

"Is the trip more important than our friendship?" K.J. demanded.

"Our friendship will always be there, but we only get one shot at this mission."

The taxis followed each other down narrow, tree-lined streets pocked with potholes and scattered with assorted scraps of windblown paper and trash. Small, simple wood-framed houses bordered the street, each sporting a wiry TV antenna on its roof. The yards were patchy at best, mostly weedy areas occasionally broken up by a spot of grass or red or gold wildflowers. When they rolled to a stop in front of a small gray and white frame structure, Rebecca exclaimed, "This is my uncle's house. It's just like I remembered it!"

Mindy looked around as she climbed out of the taxi. "So this is where you were born, Rebecca. I'll bet you're glad you moved to America."

"I'm happy I moved to America," Rebecca answered defensively, "but I'm also happy I lived here. I have relatives in both places."

While they were unloading the luggage, they heard the tinkling of a bell in the distance. The jingling sound grew louder and louder until Jeff turned around to see a Filipino man approaching them on a strange-looking bicycle. The bicycle had a big wooden box across the back of it which almost caused it to tip over. The rider was ringing the bike's bell with enough enthusiasm to draw a crowd.

"Oh, great, the ice cream man," K.J. said. His love of ice cream was legendary.

Rebecca laughed. "Hardly," she said. "It's the balut man."

"Balut? What's that?"

"Balut's a favorite in the Philippines. It's a boiled duck egg containing a partially formed duck embryo."

"Gross!" Mindy said.

"Yuck," K.J. agreed.

"Not to Filipinos," Rebecca insisted. "They crack them open, suck out the juices, and eat the animal. Shall I buy us one?"

"No way," they all quickly said.

"That's sick," Mindy added.

In a few minutes, Mr. Domingo called everyone into his living room. It was small and crowded with furniture. Two overstuffed chairs upholstered in a faded blue and gray hunting scene sat at either end of a dark blue chintz sofa, ruffled around the bottom and shiny from wear. Gray throw pillows rested on one of the sofa's padded arms. A small table at one end of the sofa supported a large, squatty round blue ceramic lamp decorated with a white lattice design and topped with a white pleated shade. At the opposite end, another table held a half dozen neatly stacked magazines and a heavy, square dark blue ashtray veined with white. A coffee table in front of the sofa had two large matching wooden bowls on top: one filled with mixed nuts and the other with cellophane-wrapped peppermints.

All the furniture sat on top of a threadbare rug swirled in a blue, brown, and gray pattern. The exposed floor around the rug was made of dark wood planks. Two straw mats lay rolled up neatly against one wall next to a pile of newspapers.

"The guys can sleep in the living room on those mats," Mr. Domingo said, pointing toward the wall. "Mindy and Rebecca will be in the small bedroom in the back, and Warren can share my room."

"That sounds great," Jeff said. "By the way, Rebecca, didn't you say you had a cousin who lives on the dump? How far are we from there?"

"Just fifteen minutes. And I've got two of them—Irene and Eduardo. She's 12 and he's 10. You'll get to meet them tomorrow when we go there."

"Have you forgotten about our equipment?" Mindy asked. "There's not much point in going there now. We can't do anything without it."

Warren reached in his pocket and pulled out a long white form. He unfolded it and shoved it toward K.J. "That reminds me. Check this list and see if I've remembered everything we had in the bag."

K.J. scanned the form carefully for a few minutes. "This looks right. We had the Canon Hi 8 camcorder, the small monitor, and an extra battery pack."

Jeff leaned over his shoulder. "What about the small microphone and the cables?"

"Oops! I almost forgot."

Warren stood up. "First thing in the morning, we'll go to the dump, then I'll take off to start working on this. While I'm gone, Jeff's in charge. If our stuff doesn't turn up soon, I'll try to find some equipment we can borrow or rent."

"What do we do until then?" Mindy asked.

"Research, Mindy. Research."

Chapter 2

Terror at Smokey Mountain

Well," Rebecca said when they got together on Monday morning, "you're all better off than I am. At least you can go home again." She had obviously been worrying about her passport a lot during the night.

K.J. came up with a worry of his own. "I'm a little bit scared to go to the dump today," he admitted. "What if I catch a disease from those people?" He stuffed rolls and jam in his mouth as he talked.

Mindy glanced up with a slight frown and said to Warren, "God will protect us, won't He?"

"Don't worry," he said. "A medical team has been running a clinic there for years. And I found out there's a hospital right across the street."

"Then why do so many children still die there?" Mindy asked.

"Well, the smoke from the burning garbage is one problem. It damages their lungs. Also, the poor food and contaminated water kill a lot of them. But that's what we're here to do something about."

"I'm still not going to get too close to anyone," K.J. said. "I'll man the camera, but from a distance."

"What camera?" Mindy snapped.

Jeff turned to Mr. Domingo. "Tell me honestly, do you think we can be of real help?"

Mr. Domingo paused before answering. "Maybe. Maybe not. Actually, we tried to rid Manila of that eyesore a few years ago. We got some of the people out of there, but they just kept moving back."

Jeff was shocked at his response. "Eyesore? What do you mean?"

"The government would like to get rid of Smokey Mountain," Mr. Domingo said flatly.

"Is that the way you feel, too?" Jeff asked.

He shrugged his shoulders. "I don't know. At least it's a good place for groups like yours to raise money for your organization."

"Raise money!" Rebecca said indignantly. "Do you think we're here to raise money for our club?"

"Well, most of the groups that come here don't really know what's going on. They don't care about those people. They come here, take pictures, and show people back home. And they make money."

"Our club isn't like that, Uncle Fernando," Rebecca said. "I can't believe you'd think I'd be a part of that for a minute."

Jeff had to wait a few minutes before he spoke. "If we do raise the $5,000 for the water project, will you make sure the money is used for that?"

Mr. Domingo cleared his throat. "We'll do what we can, but we'll have to take something out for our costs." They stared at him in disbelief.

Finally, Rebecca broke the silence. "I'm really looking forward to seeing Eduardo and Irene. It's been years since I've seen my cousins."

"Doesn't it seem funny to have relatives living on a dump?" Mindy asked.

Jeff quickly changed the subject. "Mr. Domingo suggested that we pack a lunch and take it with us. Let's do that now and get our things together. We're leaving in ten minutes."

Waiting at the jeepney stop, Jeff was amazed by all the noise and traffic. Mindy had said there were thousands of jeepneys, taxis, buses, and private cars in Manila. Right now, it seemed like they were all on this road. Finally a shiny new jeepney rolled to a stop, and the six of them boarded it.

"Boy, look at all that chrome!" K.J. yelled over the noise. "Wouldn't you love to get a peek under that hood?"

Jeff pulled out a handful of pesos and paid their fares. As they bounced along in the jeepney, he took a handkerchief out of his pocket and held it over his mouth and nose the way he saw some of the other passengers doing. He understood why. He could hardly breathe from all the fumes and dust.

"Wow, look at this!" Mindy shouted as they crossed some railroad tracks. "Do people actually live in these shacks? Is this the dump?"

"No," Rebecca said. "This is another squatter area. The people who live here make their houses out of any kind of scraps they can find. Wait till you see the ones on the dump. They're even worse."

About fifteen minutes later, Mr. Domingo signaled for the jeepney to stop and motioned for them to follow him.

They got off next to a canal which seemed to mark the boundary between Smokey Mountain and the rest of the Tondo district. Jeff had never seen such dirty water, and it was impossible to judge how deep it was. Trash floated across the surface while oily stains fanned out in shiny patches of translucent blue, green, and yellow. Insects buzzed and darted back and forth from one muddy bank to the other. Jeff smacked one on his face and wiped his hand on his jeans. The stench of rotting garbage drifted up to attack his nose.

"I think I'm going to throw up," Mindy complained. "Get a load of that filth. And take a deep breath. On second thought, don't!"

Smoke was rising from the dump, and they understood why it was called Smokey Mountain. Huge bulldozers lumbered from one place to another, their blades pushing huge piles of trash around to level the landscape. Jeff's eyes began to burn and he blinked back tears. At the same time, his eardrums pounded with the rhythm of the bulldozers.

Rebecca was eager to see her cousins. She ran ahead of the others, stopping from time to time to let them catch up. Even with her enthusiasm, it was hard for the others to press on. Mindy's face was a study in shock; K.J.'s stony; Jeff and Warren's stoic.

None of them had anticipated the scene. Jeff consoled himself with the thought that God would surely use this experience to give them all a new heart of compassion for hurting people.

Mr. Domingo stopped to talk to a stocky older man in gray and white striped overalls and a grungy white cotton undershirt. His left upper arm was decorated with a tattoo of a girl wearing a flowered lei and a long grass skirt. She seemed to hula with each ripple of his muscle. Although it was hard to hear above the noise of the monstrous machines, Mr. Domingo tried to introduce them. He told them that the man was in charge of work assignments on the dump.

Then four little boys with smudged faces and unwashed bodies came running up and tugged on Jeff's arm.

"Hi, Joe," the smallest one said, looking up into Jeff's face and dissolving in giggles.

"Hi, yourself. My name is Jeff."

"Hi, Joe," another one said.

Then, "Hi, Joe," "Hi, Joe," all around.

Rebecca explained, "Since the war, the kids call all Americans 'Joe.' You know, G.I. Joe."

They all laughed at this. "Warren and I will leave you now," Mr. Domingo said. "We'll come back and get you later. Rebecca should remember her way around, and you all have your lunches."

They were walking around meeting people and taking in the sights when Rebecca shouted for joy. She ran and threw her arms around a young boy collecting pieces of glass, and pulled him close to her.

"Eduardo, Eduardo! I can't believe it. You haven't changed that much!" she exclaimed. "How in the world are you?"

Jeff stared at the thin young man. He reminded Jeff of a poster boy for a famine relief fund. He moved clumsily in black rubber boots several sizes too large. His grimy arms hung from the frayed sleeves of a once-white T-shirt now gray, smudged with black. His loose-fitting jeans were gathered around his small waist by a rope belt. His delicate features were too sharply defined in a gaunt face. His medium-brown hair, with a mind of its own, stuck out in a dozen different cowlicks, making his head resemble a small porcupine. But his soulful dark eyes radiated an amazing warmth and happiness.

"I'm fine," he said, and his wide, toothy grin served as proof.

It seemed inconceivable to Jeff that someone as young as this ten year old should have to spend most of his hours working on a dump.

Rebecca introduced him to the team and explained why they had come. "Do you have to work today?" she asked.

"Yes, we work every day in the summer when school is out. I need to get back soon, but I'll show you around a little."

Jeff walked ahead of the others. He was interested to see some children happily throwing litter at one another just as other children might have tossed a ball. As they scrambled around, they stirred up their environment so much that their tiny forms were almost lost in clouds of smoldering trash.

Eduardo led them to an area where huge bulldozers attacked piles of rotting garbage, transferring it from one location to another in an attempt to level the terrain. They seemed to be battling a lost cause as large trucks pulled up periodically and dumped out new refuse. The heap grew higher and higher.

"Those bulldozers really scare me," K.J. admitted. "Doesn't anyone ever get hurt?"

"Once in a while. But there's a hospital across the street," Eduardo said matter-of-factly.

"I'm checking out some facts for our video," Mindy said. "Do you mind if I ask you how much you make each day?"

"Our family gets three dollars a day if everyone works." Before he left them, Eduardo thanked them all. "My parents will be very grateful that you have come to help us."

When he was gone, Mindy complained, "This place smells awful, and I'm dying of thirst. I wish the water system were already working."

K.J. chimed in, "Yeah, me, too. Do you think we could get anything to drink around here?"

Rebecca pointed to a makeshift shack. "That looks like a store. Maybe we could get some Cokes over there."

K.J. looked skeptical. "I'm sure we're going to find a store selling soft drinks in a dump!"

But Rebecca was right. They enjoyed their refreshments while trying to talk above the constant roar of heavy equipment.

Jeff could see Eduardo way in the distance picking away with a little scavenging hook. "Your cousin is an amazing kid. Where are his parents?"

"He told me they're away visiting some relatives today. His older sister, Irene, is the only one home."

Suddenly, an ominous quiet descended upon them. Everything seemed to stop at once in response to some unheard signal. Crowds of people moved in the same direction. First in slow motion, and then running, they gathered at the base of a huge mountain of garbage.

Screams pierced the silence.

The team ran in the direction of the screams. As they got closer, Jeff felt terror crawling up his back.

"What happened?" he yelled when he got to the edge of the crowd.

"One of the bulldozers hit a kid. Looks like he's hurt real bad."

Jeff stood on his toes and saw a limp body crumpled on the ground. He blinked his eyes. He blinked again. He didn't want to believe what he had seen. He closed his eyes and said a quick prayer: "Oh, God, please, no."

When he turned around to face the team, he had to admit the truth.

"It's Eduardo!"

Chapter 3

Life or Death

Is there a doctor around?" Rebecca pleaded hysterically.

She was surrounded by a sea of horrified faces. "Not today," someone shouted back. "He's working in another part of Tondo today."

"We've got to get him to a hospital right away," Rebecca said emphatically.

A young girl who had been elbowing her way through the crowd finally made it to the front and fell sobbing next to Eduardo. If anything, the girl's arms and legs were even thinner than Eduardo's. She had on a long blue and white checked sundress that was several sizes too big for her and had been torn and patched more than once. She wore what had once been white sandals, but were now pieces of leather held together by the barest of straps. Her soft, wavy brown hair fell across Eduardo's face. When she raised her head, Jeff noticed a striking resemblance between the two. Her large, round brown eyes filled with tears as she begged the crowd for help.

Rebecca gasped. "It's Irene. His sister."

"Somebody do something quick," Irene cried. "He's bleeding badly."

While everyone else stood frozen, Rebecca ripped off a piece of the hem of her dress, folded it, and pressed it against Eduardo's head to stop the flow of blood. Then the man who had driven the bulldozer stepped forward and scooped up Eduardo in his arms, literally pulling him out of his sister's grasp.

"I'm sure he'll be fine," Mindy lied to Rebecca.

The crowd parted to let the driver through, then followed at a respectful distance as he carried Eduardo down the long narrow pathway that followed the canal. With every step he took, Jeff said a quick prayer: "Lord, don't let him die."

The procession zigzagged down the mountain and then across the busy street, fearlessly dodging cars, motorcycles, buses, jeepneys, and bikes. Tires screeched and horns blared as careening vehicles attempted to dodge the desperate little band intent on their emergency mission. Jeff wondered if they would all survive the trip to the other side.

But they made it. And once safely inside the hospital, a new problem appeared: would-be patients leaned against every wall and sprawled across every bench and chair, with no medical personnel in sight.

"Oh, no," K.J. gasped. "Is this their busy day?"

"It sure doesn't look like our hospitals in Los Angeles," Mindy declared.

The hospital was a narrow, gray concrete five-story building. The double front doors opened onto a large waiting room with stark white walls and a shiny beige vinyl floor. Brown molded plastic chairs with aluminum legs and long, hard wooden benches were randomly scattered around the room next to small wooden tables. Three sparse, live plants in white ceramic pots tried in vain to provide relief from the sterile decor. They were helped somewhat by pictures of brightly colored flowers on two of the walls and uneven stacks of magazines on the floor.

A wooden counter in the middle of the room separated the waiting area from an office and examining rooms. The back wall had an archway leading to a long corridor with many doors. To the right of the archway was a bank of three elevators.

Behind the counter sat two wooden desks with brown vinyl swivel chairs tucked in the center of them. A multitude of files, charts, and papers were piled atop each desk. Two examining rooms were visible behind the desks, with two sheet-draped gurneys in each. One room was already crammed with people, two of them lying on the gurneys.

But in the other room, Jeff spotted an empty bed. An elderly gentleman had already taken up residence on the other one. Jeff motioned for the driver to lay Eduardo down in there.

The driver looked apologetically at Irene. "I have to go now or I'll lose my job. It was an accident. I never even saw him. I hope he'll be okay."

Mindy, Rebecca, and Irene intertwined their arms in a circle of grief as tears spilled down their cheeks. Jeff felt a lump in his throat, and noticed that K.J.'s eyes were larger and his complexion paler than usual. It was amazing that Eduardo could become so important to them all so fast.

There wasn't a doctor or nurse in sight. After what was probably just a few minutes, but seemed like an eternity, Mindy's patience gave out.

"Where are all the doctors, anyway?" she said in a loud, rude voice. "This is supposed to be a hospital. I'm going to start screaming in about one minute if someone doesn't show up soon."

Rebecca took her hand. "The medical system here is very different from that in the States. People are used to waiting for everything. Even after the doctor shows up, we'll have to go somewhere and buy the supplies he needs."

"You've got to be kidding!" K.J. exclaimed.

"No, I'm afraid not. We'll need some money to pay for them. And some of us should stay here with Eduardo and Irene."

A few minutes later, Jeff decided to take matters into his own hands and go find help. He walked down the long corridor, twisting his head to look in open doors on both sides as he passed them. Every room was crowded with people and he was amazed to see that some beds held two or three people each.

When he was unable to find any hospital personnel, he reluctantly returned to the group. "I don't understand why there are so few doctors and so many patients here. There's even more than one person to a bed," he said in dismay.

Rebecca nodded. "In this country, families are allowed to stay with sick relatives as long as they occupy only one bed."

"Boy, remind me never to get sick in Manila," K.J. muttered under his breath.

Everyone jumped up when a doctor and two nurses finally entered the waiting room, and they began a waving and shouting match to get the doctor's attention. He walked straight into the room where Eduardo was stretched out, and picked up his wrist to take his pulse. "I'm Dr. Sanchez," he said without meeting anyone's eyes. "This one looks like he needs some help right away."

Dr. Sanchez had thinning brown hair brushed to one side. His round, rimless glasses hooked over large, protruding ears. When he looked up, they saw that his deep-set eyes looked tired and soulful. He was wearing a much-washed green scrub suit and crepe-soled shoes. He took the stethoscope from around his neck and listened to Eduardo's chest. Jeff estimated the doctor to be much younger than he looked.

"What happened to him?" Dr. Sanchez asked.

By this time, Irene was sobbing too hard to answer him.

"He was hit by a bulldozer," Rebecca explained. "Almost half an hour ago."

Finally, Irene found her voice. "Please help him. Please. Please. He's my brother."

The doctor used his thumb and forefinger to open one of Eduardo's eyes. "We'll do what we can. First, we'll need some X-rays. All of you, wait here."

He motioned for one of the nurses to wheel Eduardo out of the room.

Jeff gathered the group in a circle and had them join hands. "We need to pray," he said.

"Lord, You're the One Who made Eduardo," he led off. "Please perform a miracle in his life. And please be with Irene. Give her Your peace."

"I'm sorry for my bad attitude," K.J. said with bowed head. "I didn't want to go on this trip when I heard it was just to an old dump. Forgive me. I feel like a jerk."

Mindy squeezed his hand. "Please forgive me, too. All I've done is complain since I left Los Angeles."

Rebecca added, "I'm sorry because I really didn't want to come back here. I wanted to forget about this part of my life."

She put her arms around Irene. "But God has put a whole new love in my heart for my people, and now I'm glad I came. I know there's a reason I'm here. I'm just not sure what it is yet."

Jeff continued his prayer: "Please, Lord, let the things we have experienced change all our hearts. Fill us with Your love for everyone we meet. And be with Eduardo. We know he's very important to You, and he's become important to us, too."

Jeff felt like God had already been at work in

Manila since their arrival. He sensed that God was in the process of turning them into even more of a team. Almost a mighty army.

Mindy wiped her glasses on her shirt. "Boy, I don't remember ever crying so much in one day. I can't wait to go back to Smokey Mountain now. I sure won't let the dirt and heat bother me anymore."

Just then, Dr. Sanchez came back in the room with a very grim look on his face.

"Where are the boy's parents?" he asked.

"They went to visit some friends today," Irene said. "They left me to take care of him." And then she began to cry again.

"Your brother took a bad blow to the head. The cut isn't too bad, but he's suffered a severe concussion."

"How bad?" Mindy asked.

"We won't know for a while," the doctor said.

"Is there anything we can do?" Rebecca asked.

"Try saying a few prayers," he said somewhat flippantly.

"We've already done that," Jeff answered.

"I'll let you know what's going on as soon as the test results come back. In the meantime, somebody needs to contact his parents."

Irene said, "There's no way. We'll just have to hope they hear about what happened and come home."

They almost bumped into each other pacing around, waiting for the doctor to return. Occasionally, someone would stop to wonder aloud how Eduardo was doing. Jeff looked at his watch. It was 2:30 in the afternoon. They had only been in the Philippines one day, and already so much had happened.

After they had been waiting another hour, an older couple dressed in simple cotton work clothes dashed into the room. Irene immediately burst into tears and ran over to embrace them. Then she introduced everyone to her parents. Jeff was pleased to note that they understood English.

"We're very sorry," Jeff said. "We're here to help any way we can."

Rebecca assured them, "Eduardo is a tough boy. With lots of prayer, he's going to pull through."

"We've all been praying for him," K.J. said. "That's at least one thing we can do."

When the doctor came back, he expressed relief that Eduardo's parents were there. He addressed them directly, "Eduardo has suffered a serious concussion. He's in a deep coma. I'm sorry to have to tell you that we can't pick up any brain waves."

"What does that mean exactly?" Irene asked.

The doctor cleared his throat, then answered, "I don't think there's much we can do for him."

"You mean he might die?" Rebecca asked incredulously.

He turned to Eduardo's parents. "Our hospital isn't equipped to handle this kind of trauma," he said. "I'm not sure any hospital is. If he's truly brain dead, it's only a matter of time."

Chapter 4

A Dirty Plan

They hadn't been prepared for news this bad.

"We're not going to give up," Jeff said.

"Right. We'll just take him to another hospital," Mindy agreed.

Eduardo's mother started crying. "You don't understand. We have no money. We can't afford to move him."

Jeff looked at his watch. "Warren will be back soon. He'll think of something."

"I'll stay with Eduardo tonight," Irene offered. "My mom and dad have to work tomorrow."

K.J. jumped up from the bench where he had sat

down to rest. "I've got another idea. I'll take Eduardo's place on the dump tomorrow. In fact, why don't all of us work there so his parents can stay at the hospital?"

"You mean dig through garbage?" Mindy asked.

K.J. smiled. "Yeah. Just think of it as research."

Warren came running in the door breathing heavily. "I just heard what happened. How's Eduardo?"

Jeff filled him in on the boy's condition and finished by telling him K.J.'s idea.

Warren raised his eyebrows but made no comment. He turned to Jeff and Mindy and said, "I called your parents this morning to tell them about the theft. I'll call them back to see if they can come up with any ideas about how to help Eduardo. With all their connections, they might be able to do something."

"You mean like raise some money?" Jeff asked.

"Maybe," said Warren. "That's one possibility. Let's think about it. Anyway, we have to wait. They'd be asleep right now."

"What about Rebecca's passport?" Mindy asked. "Will she be able to go home with us?"

"I spent the whole morning just filing a report about the camera case. Tomorrow, I'll tackle the passport. Rebecca and I have to go to the embassy together for that."

"What about the tickets?" K.J. asked.

"I already know we'll have to buy some new ones. We'll worry about getting a refund from the airline when we get back."

"What about our working on the dump?" K.J. persisted.

Warren frowned. "I'm not so sure about that. If anyone does work on the dump, I'll have to make sure it's in a safe area."

K.J. assured him, "Don't worry. After today, I'm sure none of us will get close to any bulldozers."

Mindy and Rebecca embraced Irene, and Jeff gave a hug to her parents before they left. He promised to think of a way to get some help for Eduardo.

"Thanks, and God bless you," Irene said. Her parents nodded. "You all run along. What you need now is a good meal and some rest. We'll stay with Eduardo."

"You're right, Irene," Warren admitted. "A nice warm bed and something to eat sounds awfully good right now."

On Tuesday morning, Mr. Domingo dressed and left before the rest of them got up.

After making their own breakfast, Jeff, Mindy, and K.J. headed for the dump while Rebecca and Warren took off for the embassy.

"I feel good about what we're going to do today," K.J. said as they rode in the jeepney.

"This was one of your better ideas, K.J.," Jeff congratulated him. "This is the kind of thing that Jesus would do."

Mindy leaned over and said, "That's right. We can just think of it this way: When Jesus came into this world, it was just a big garbage dump. He changed everything when He worked with other people."

K.J.'s eyes got big. "Yeah. Now I feel like Jesus can work through us. I never would have believed I could get so excited about working on a dump."

Their first stop was at the hospital to check on Eduardo. They were happy to learn that he was conveniently in the first room on the right down the hall off the waiting room. But they were discouraged when they found out that he had improved none from the day before.

Since they obviously couldn't do anything for Eduardo, they decided to go on to the dump. As they were making their way along the canal, Jeff said, "I overheard one of the nurses talking about a medical team that was trying to carry water to the people on the dump during a typhoon. One girl on the team missed the place where you're supposed to cross and fell in the canal."

"You mean she fell into that slime?" K.J. asked, peering into the murky water and wrinkling his nose.

"Yeah, but she probably didn't think it was as bad as we do. I understand that some people actually bathe their kids in that water."

"That's disgusting," Mindy said. "I never knew we had it so good."

When they came to the house where the man in charge of work assignments lived, Mindy knocked at the door.

"You're back again," he said, opening the door.

"We've come to replace Eduardo and his parents for the day."

The man's eyes twinkled; and he invited them inside. K.J. couldn't take his eyes off the tattoo of the Hawaiian girl until Mindy punched him and gave him a stern warning stare.

"Actually, a friend of Eduardo's parents came here and told me you'd be showing up, but I wasn't sure you'd make it. The friend brought some work clothes for you to wear."

Once they had changed clothes, Jeff, Mindy, and K.J. headed out in the direction the man told them to go. They discussed their assignments as they walked.

Eduardo's job had been to find broken glass while his parents looked for strips of plastic and old bones.

"What do you suppose they use bones for?" Mindy asked.

"I was told they grind them up to make fertilizer," Jeff answered.

"And what about the glass and strips of plastic?" K.J. asked.

"The glass is ground and the plastic is recycled. Other people on the dump buy it and resell it. It's like a giant flea market. Nothing goes to waste."

They passed by some kids playing, and Jeff pointed out that the kids had their T-shirts pulled up over their heads. "That's to protect their lungs."

"Don't expect me to do that," Mindy said indignantly.

"Whatever works is okay with me," K.J. said.

When they got to their work site, Jeff handed everyone an L-shaped hook used for scavenging.

Then they divided up the bags they had brought and went to work.

"I can't believe they work three shifts here," Mindy said, sticking close by the boys.

"Day and night."

"I didn't know garbage was such big business," K.J. admitted.

"Please be careful," Jeff warned. "Rebecca told me garbage can explode. It can cave in, too."

They spent the morning filling their bags, working in an area away from the huge bulldozers. But there was no way to escape the noise, smell, or dirt of the dump. After a while, their skin was filthy and they were coughing with almost every breath. Now it was easy to understand why the children had covered their heads with their T-shirts.

"I'd give anything to jump in a nice cool swimming pool right now," K.J. joked. "Just think how many there are in Los Angeles alone."

"Well, I, for one, will never complain again about having to take a shower." Mindy said.

Everyone quickly agreed when Jeff suggested stopping for lunch. They cleared a spot next to where a group of other workers was eating and sat on the ground. Jeff was proud of how well Mindy and K.J. mingled with the Filipinos. They kept trying to strike up a conversation, and smiled and made hand gestures when their English failed. It was as if God were turning them all into one big family.

When they were ready to go back to work, Jeff saw Rebecca walking along the canal.

"I've come to help," she said as she approached. "How's it going?"

"Well," Jeff said, "We're a little dirty, but doing fine."

"How's Eduardo?" Mindy asked.

"Not good. I stopped by the hospital. He's still in a coma."

"What about your passport?" K.J. asked.

"Also not good. We've got to fill out all kinds of papers and take them back in. It'll be a miracle if I get to go back home with all of you next Monday. Warren is still working on the return tickets, too. He said you're still in charge, Jeff."

Rebecca offered to help them, and Jeff assigned her the job of searching for bottle caps.

They worked diligently side by side all afternoon. Jeff kept thinking that if he had written the script for this week, he would never have written it the way it was going so far. It was obvious that God was in charge, and only He knew what the ending would be.

Jeff was greatly relieved when he looked at his watch and saw that it was almost quitting time. His relief was short lived, though, when he heard a loud scream and recognized the voice.

By the time Jeff reached his friend, blood was gushing out of K.J.'s right arm like a fountain.

Chapter 5

Mysterious Pictures

Let's get him to the clinic quick," Rebecca said, turning pale. "But first, we'd better try to stop the bleeding."

Mindy spotted a pile of newspapers and grabbed some of the cleanest looking ones to wrap around K.J.'s arm, gently applying pressure.

"Follow me," a Filipino man volunteered. "The clinic's real close."

Jeff put an arm around K.J.'s waist and helped him along the path to the clinic. "What happened?" Jeff asked.

"I'm not sure," K.J. said. "I was digging through the garbage, and I must have cut myself on a piece of glass or something."

When they arrived at the clinic, they couldn't find any medical workers, just other waiting patients. In desperation, Mindy rummaged around until she found some clean strips of white cotton in a drawer, and Rebecca came up with a bottle of alcohol to cleanse the wound.

"This is going to hurt some," Mindy warned K.J., winding the strips tightly around his arm.

"It's okay. I can take it." K.J. grimaced and clenched his fists.

Then they decided they had better go to the hospital for more treatment. When they were getting ready to leave, Jeff noticed that Mindy kept turning a dirty envelope over and over in her hands.

"What's that?" he asked.

"I don't know," Mindy said. "It fell out of the newspapers that were around K.J.'s arm. It looks like it hasn't been opened yet."

"People have already gone through the garbage at the dump several times, so it's obviously trash," Rebecca said. "The address is all smudged, so we can't send it on."

"Well, open it," K.J. said. "Maybe there's some money inside. We could sure use some with all these unplanned medical expenses."

The Filipino man who had led them to the clinic watched with interest as Mindy tore open the envelope and pulled out its contents.

"Oh, rats," she said. "No money. Just some pictures and a letter."

When she handed the pictures to Jeff, the man leaned over Jeff's shoulder to get a better look. His eyes grew large with fright, and he started edging toward the door.

"This is very, very dangerous. Get rid of those right now!" he said, then ran out the door.

"Wonder what's wrong with him?" K.J. muttered.

"I don't know, but I think we'd better find out," Jeff said. "First, let's get you to the hospital."

He handed everything back to Mindy, and she stuffed the letter and pictures back in the envelope and dropped it in her pocket.

All the way to the hospital, Jeff kept thinking about the Filipino man's reaction. What could possibly be so dangerous about a few pictures?

Once again, they had to dodge traffic on the busy road with an injured person in tow.

"Well, at least we can visit Irene and her parents while we're at the hospital," Mindy said.

"I'd like to do it under different circumstances, thank you," K.J. said.

This time they were fortunate that the waiting room was almost empty. Dr. Sanchez was sitting on the edge of one of the desks talking with a nurse. He recognized them right away and came to greet them.

"Aren't you the ones who brought that boy with the head injury in here yesterday?"

"Yes, sir. This time we've got someone with a bad

cut," Mindy said. "He got hurt working on the dump."

"I should think you would stay away from that dump."

The doctor walked K.J to a sink and took off the bandages. He examined the wound closely. "He'll need stitches. I'll give you a list of supplies to get for me at the pharmacy."

K.J. stammered, "I can't believe this. I just sit here bleeding while you guys go shopping!"

Dr. Sanchez broke into a grin for the first time. He took off his glasses and wiped them on his scrub suit. He sat down on a chair, stretched his legs out in front of him, and breathed a deep sigh. "You'll be okay. It's just the way we do things here."

"I hope we don't bring back the wrong stuff," Mindy teased playfully. She shook her head dramatically and her ponytail flopped from ear to ear.

"Mindy, I'm in no mood for jokes," K.J. snapped.

Jeff and Mindy decided to leave Rebecca with K.J. while they went for the supplies. While they waited for the pharmacist to assemble everything on the doctor's list, Jeff said to Mindy, "Let's have another look at those pictures. I want to see why that man was so frightened."

"I sure can't see why," she said as she pulled the pictures out.

Together they studied them. They seemed innocent enough. There was a picture of two men huddled together over a table. There was another one of the same men getting out of a dark, late-model car together, and finally a picture of the heavier man handing what looked like a large manila envelope to the other one. An official-looking brick building was in the background of this picture, but it was impossible to decipher the writing on the building.

"Mindy," Jeff said, "what does the letter say?"

"How should I know? It's written in some language. It's probably Tagalog. We'll have to ask Rebecca if she remembers enough Tagalog to read it. Or wait until we see Irene again."

"Can't you make out any of it?" Jeff asked.

"Of course not. But the letter must have something to do with the pictures. All we know is that they sure scared that man at the clinic."

Jeff said, "We'll ask Mr. Domingo or Irene to explain this. Maybe they'll recognize the men."

When the pharmacist presented them with the bag of supplies and the bill, Jeff unzipped his money pouch and paid for everything. Then they hurried back to the hospital.

As soon as they entered the waiting room, Jeff saw Rebecca sitting at a little table in the corner, deep in conversation with the doctor. He immediately surmised what they were discussing. Rebecca was a new convert to Christianity and jumped at every opportunity to share her testimony. The doctor was either a willing listener or a captive audience.

Mindy walked over and handed Dr. Sanchez the bag and he inspected its contents. He made sure everything was there, even the needle and thread.

"Rebecca was telling me that you're part of a club," Dr. Sanchez said.

"That's right," Jeff said. "The Reel Kids Club."

While the doctor scrubbed his hands, he continued talking to Jeff over his shoulder. "I'd like to hear more about it sometime. Rebecca says that her life changed when she found a personal relationship with Jesus Christ."

"That's for sure," Jeff said. "How do you feel about what she said?"

He shrugged his shoulders. "I know a lot of people who believe in God. In fact, I was raised in church, but I've never heard religion explained the way she did just now."

The doctor examined K.J.'s arm, then said, "K.J., I'm going to give you a shot to deaden the pain so I can stitch up your arm." Everyone looked away, including K.J.

Just then Irene walked in the room and gasped, "I heard you were here. What happened?"

"Another accident," Jeff explained.

Her eyes filled with tears and she began wringing her hands. "Another one. I don't think I can take much more. Eduardo is no better. In fact, I think he's even worse."

"What can we do?" Jeff asked. "I'm sure that Warren won't give up until he reaches my parents, but I don't know if anyone can raise enough money to help him on such short notice."

The doctor looked up from stitching K.J.'s cut.

"I'm very sorry. I wish there were more I could do. We're limited here. Eduardo needs to be in a hospital in Metro Manila."

"I still say he's going to be okay," Mindy said with conviction.

"Ouch," K.J. cried. "What happened to the pain killer?"

"This will sting some, but you'll be good as new when we're done," the doctor assured him. When he finished, he turned to the group.

"I'd like to hear more about this personal relationship you say you have with Jesus. I've not heard anything quite like that before, but I'm in the business of healing people, and I'm always interested in anything that makes a person feel better."

"Jesus is a healer, too," Jeff said boldly. "Of body, soul, and spirit."

"Where did you get that idea?" the doctor asked.

Jeff was more than happy to relate the story that he had shared many times before. He told the doctor about how he'd nearly died in a car accident when he was much younger. Everyone had given up on him then, just like they had on Eduardo now. But Jesus had appeared to Jeff in his hospital room and healed him. The experience had changed his life.

"That's why I joined this club. Our faith is why all of us are members. 'R-e-e-l' Kids really stands for 'r-e-a-l' kids. We try to make a difference in the world. The club gives us a chance to travel to different countries and share our stories about Jesus."

Mindy couldn't keep her mouth shut any longer. "Doesn't it seem strange to you that circumstances have led us here twice already? I suppose you think it's an accident that you've been the one to help us both times. Well, I don't think so. I think God sent us here deliberately to tell you about Him. Shall we pray about it?"

"Wait a minute. Not so fast, young lady." Dr. Sanchez held up a hand. "You have my curiosity up, but I want to think about what you've all said."

Jeff offered, "Please feel free to ask us anything you want to know. I'm sure we'll be seeing you again."

"Well, I'll see you on Saturday for sure. I want to check your stitches again before you go back to the States."

After the doctor left, they all rallied around Irene to offer her support. Jeff said, "Irene, we'd like to pray for Eduardo and your family."

"Oh, that would be great. I feel so helpless. And I'd like to hear more about what you were telling the doctor."

They followed Irene into Eduardo's room. It was a large room filled with beds, patients, medical paraphernalia, and people milling around. Eduardo's bed was curtained off from the rest of the room. His parents were leaning over the bed whispering to him. His mother held his hand up to her wrinkled face and brushed it with a kiss. She seemed to have aged tremendously in just the short time since they had last seen her.

"Daddy and Mama, the team is here to pray for Eduardo. Jeff, if you don't mind, please explain to them what you were telling the doctor before you pray."

Jeff, Mindy, K.J., and Rebecca took turns talking to Irene and her parents about the Lord. They had a lot of questions about what it meant to be a follower of Jesus. Irene asked the most.

"Maybe this all happened just so we could hear about your Jesus," she finally said.

"So do you want us to pray with you to receive Jesus?" Jeff asked.

"I'm ready," Irene said.

"Me, too," her mother softly agreed.

"I need to think about it some more," her father said.

They prayed with each one separately. Jeff was especially sensitive when it was the father's turn. He simply asked that God would prepare his heart to receive Jesus. Then Jeff suggested that they all pray for Eduardo.

He closed his eyes and led the group in a simple prayer: "Jesus, thank You for receiving new members into Your family today. We ask that You would touch Eduardo and heal him. Amen."

When Jeff opened his eyes, he noticed that Eduardo's leg was moving slightly. He pointed it out excitedly to the others. Each of them now made a concentrated effort to rouse Eduardo, but there was no more response.

"Don't worry," Mindy assured them. "God has given us a sign. Eduardo's going to get better. We just have to wait."

The team said their goodbyes, and Jeff asked Irene to step out in the hall with them. Mindy pulled the envelope out of her pocket and handed it to Irene.

"Irene, we found these pictures and this letter at the dump today. Can you read this?"

Irene started reading the letter, and her mouth dropped open. She let out a long whistle.

"What's wrong?" Mindy asked.

Irene raised her eyebrows, and her large brown eyes looked even larger. "This letter was written by a man who worked for the mayor. He disappeared last week. The police think he's been kidnapped. This letter is probably the reason."

She put one of the pictures on top of the others and pointed to the face of the man receiving the envelope. "This is Napoleon Laurel, the mayor's assistant. And I've seen the other man's picture in the paper a lot. He's one of the main gangsters in the Philippines. He's involved in drugs, prostitution, and murder. I don't know what he and Mr. Laurel were doing in these pictures, but it couldn't be anything innocent.

"This letter was written to an official, telling him about Mr. Laurel being corrupt," she said. "That's why the man who wrote it disappeared. If someone finds out you have these, you could be in a whole lot of trouble."

Chapter 6

Dangerous Leak

Who else knows about this?" Irene demanded.

Jeff wrinkled his forehead. "Well, let's see. The Filipino man who took us to the clinic is the only one I can think of. When he saw the pictures, he ran out of the room."

Irene sank into a chair. "What if he decides to try to make some money by telling Mr. Laurel that you have these?"

"Are you saying you think the mayor's corrupt, too?" Jeff asked.

"No, he's supposed to be a good man, but I don't know about everyone who works for him. Some of our past leaders were really crooked. Especially when Ferdinand and Imelda Marcos were in power."

"Yeah. I remember when I was studying about the Philippines that I was really shocked at how much stuff they took from your country," Mindy said. "We're talking billions of dollars."

Irene looked down at the floor. "It's hard to know who to believe. When you can't trust the people at the top, corruption filters down to everybody. And our bad economy only adds to the problem."

"Let's get rid of these pictures right now. We'll take them to the police," K.J. suggested.

"Not so fast," Irene urged. "Remember what I said. We need to make sure we get them into the right hands. Someone we can trust."

"In the meantime, we'll have to think of something to do with them," Jeff said. "We can't just leave them laying around for someone else to find."

This was something they all agreed on. Irene handed the envelope back to Jeff like a hot potato. "You take it. I don't want it. You be responsible for it until we find the right person to give it to."

"Why don't we just throw it away and forget the whole thing?" K.J. suggested.

"No, we have to do the right thing. The man who wrote the letter is obviously in a lot of danger. And if a government official is really crooked, he needs to be exposed," Jeff said staunchly.

K.J. persisted. "I didn't volunteer to come here and get killed. Why don't we just let the people of Manila solve their own problems?"

"We'll discuss it with Warren before we make any decisions," Jeff said.

"Wait a minute," Rebecca said. She was jumping up and down with excitement. "We're forgetting something. We're forgetting that my uncle works for the government. He must know the mayor. We'll just give these to him."

"Whatever we do, let's do it fast," K.J. urged. "My head is throbbing as much as my arm right now."

On their way back to Mr. Domingo's house, their jeepney whipped into a busy intersection, and it looked like vehicles were coming at them from every direction. Jeff heard horns blasting, a loud screeching of tires, and a huge thud accompanied by the sound of scraping metal.

Jeff grabbed for Mindy, only to have her slip out of his grasp and onto the floor. K.J. clutched his injured arm and yelled in pain as he was slammed against the side of the vehicle. Somehow Rebecca managed to stay on her seat. Great clouds of dust surrounded their jeepney and the one it had collided with, but both of them managed to stay upright.

Once Jeff made sure everyone was all right, he took a minute to think about their situation. He looked at his watch and saw that it was 7:30. And only Tuesday night. He wondered how so many things could have gone wrong so quickly. He wondered if they were victims of some sort of spiritual warfare.

It was a minute before he could find his voice. "Are you guys okay?"

"I'm ready to go back to L.A.," K.J. admitted.

"It's okay," Rebecca assured them. "Fender benders are pretty routine around Manila."

"Fender bender!" K.J. protested. "We could have been killed!"

Rebecca just smiled reassuringly. "Well, one thing's for sure. We have to get off and catch another jeepney now."

"Can anything else go wrong?" Mindy lamented.

"Don't even ask," K.J. pleaded.

They were still shaken when they walked up the sidewalk to Mr. Domingo's front porch. Inside, they found Warren alone and on the telephone. He waved at them and looked shocked as he pointed to K.J.'s bandaged arm. They waited around the kitchen table until he was off the phone.

"What in the world happened to you, K.J.?"

"I had an accident on the dump."

Jeff filled him in on the details.

"I'm sorry you had to handle all this," Warren apologized to Jeff. "I'm still working on our return tickets. I was talking to the airline when you came in."

"Jeff's doing a great job," Mindy said proudly. "You put the right man in charge."

Jeff handed Warren the envelope with the letter and pictures in it, and told him how they found them. He also told him Irene's warning. Warren slowly turned the pictures over in his hands. He stared at the letter. He was silent for a few minutes.

"Something about this troubles me," he finally said. "I can't explain it, but I have a strange feeling that we were meant to find this envelope."

"That's funny," Jeff said. "I feel the same way."

"I'd like to know more about this kidnapped man," Warren said. "Did Irene say it happened just last week?"

Rebecca rose and headed for the stack of papers in the corner of the room. "I think I saw something about it in one of these newspapers. They're in English, so you can read it for yourself."

She thumbed through the papers while everyone sat quietly and watched. Then she pulled one newspaper out of the pile. "Here it is! Here's a story about it. It happened last Thursday."

"Look, the story's circled," Mindy pointed out. "Do you suppose your uncle knew the man?"

"Probably. His department is connected to the mayor's office."

"He couldn't have had anything to do with it, could he?" Mindy asked cautiously.

"Of course not!" Rebecca was indignant. "My uncle's worked for the government for years. He's very respected here."

"So was the mayor's assistant," K.J. said quietly.

"Are you accusing my uncle of being a criminal?" Rebecca asked angrily.

"I'm sorry. It's just that everything's gotten kind of crazy," K.J. apologized.

"Well, one thing's certain," Warren said after he read the article. "We have to keep the envelope in a safe place until we find the right person to give it to."

"What's a safe place?" Mindy asked.

"I'll think of one," Warren said as he shoved the envelope in his pocket. "It might be better if you guys don't know where it is, though."

After everyone else had gone to bed, Jeff and Warren stayed up discussing what they should do.

"What's the latest on Rebecca's passport?" Jeff asked.

"We're supposed to hear tomorrow."

They stopped talking when Mr. Domingo came in. He wasn't smiling his usual smile, and his eyes seemed hard and cold.

"Good evening, Mr. Domingo." Jeff tried to sound friendly.

"What's good about it?" the man snapped.

"I'm sorry, sir. Did you have a bad day?"

Without another word, Mr. Domingo walked straight to his room and slammed the door.

The sun woke Jeff before his alarm went off. It was Wednesday already, and nothing had been done on the video. In fact, matters got worse each day.

K.J. still had his head buried in his pillow, and Jeff felt a pang of sympathy when he looked at his bandaged arm.

He crept over to the door to Mr. Domingo's room and cautiously inched it open. He peeked inside, hoping Warren was awake. The bathroom door was open and Warren was standing at the sink, shaving. Mr. Domingo was nowhere in sight.

"You're up early," Jeff said.

"Mr. Domingo got up about five o'clock and left. I'm surprised you didn't hear him. Something's wrong, and I'm going to find out what."

"He's sure one busy man," Jeff observed. Warren didn't respond.

Warren pulled on a bright blue and green checked shirt and said, "I'd like for us to go to Smokey Mountain this morning to plan the taping."

Jeff looked at him excitedly. "You mean they found our equipment?"

"No, afraid not. I checked with the police station a few minutes ago. There's a new twist. They think somebody knew we were bringing video equipment with us before we arrived."

"So what does that mean? Do you think the job was set up?"

"Quite possibly. That equipment could bring a lot of money here. Or maybe there was another reason...."

"This gets more interesting all the time," Jeff said.

"Get the others up," Warren said. "We need to get going. I'll go with you to the dump first, and then to the embassy to see about Rebecca's passport."

"We should also visit Eduardo," Jeff said. "There's a doctor we need to talk to."

When they got off the jeepney near the dump, Irene was already waiting for them.

"Hurry! Hurry!" she cried, panic registered in her red, swollen eyes.

"What's wrong?" Jeff asked in alarm.

She wiped at her eyes. "I'm so scared. I can't quit crying. When I was on my way to the hospital this morning, I overheard two men talking about some pictures. I'm almost sure they were talking about the ones you found. And, what's more, I heard them mention Jeff's name and Rebecca's uncle."

"What exactly does that mean?" Mindy asked.

"It means you're in a lot of danger. Somebody knows you have the pictures, and they must know where you're staying. They'll come looking for you. Somebody is going to want those pictures back real bad."

Chapter 7

Angry Host

Jeff turned to the others and shook his head. "How did we get in this mess anyway?"

"I guess I should have been more careful on the dump," K.J. laughed.

"This is no time for your silly jokes," Mindy snapped.

"Now, let's just stay calm," Warren said. "I still think God has a purpose in all of this. We just don't know what it is yet."

Irene stopped crying, and her face lit up. "I've got a great idea. I have some friends who live in that squatter area we passed on the way to the dump. I'll bet they'd let you hide out there."

"I think we're okay for now, but we'll keep it in mind," Warren said.

Rebecca interrupted. "I don't think we should go to the dump now. It's too dangerous. Let's go visit Eduardo, then head back to my uncle's house and ask him what to do."

"I'm not so sure about that," Jeff said hesitantly. "He's seems very upset about something."

"Maybe he's just tired of house guests," Warren said.

Rebecca looked puzzled. "He's changed since I moved to the States. He used to like having company a lot. I don't know. Maybe he's just getting older."

Jeff nodded. "Maybe. Anyway, let's go visit Eduardo and then think about our next move."

The group formed a circle around Eduardo's bed and once again took turns praying for him.

Mindy couldn't take her eyes off Eduardo's thin, pale face. He looked so sweet and vulnerable, his eyes tightly closed and his spiky hair fanning out on the pillow. "He moved his leg yesterday. I know he did. Jeff said so. Why doesn't he do it today?"

"Well, I can't answer that," Irene said. "But the doctor said it's all right to leave him here for a while. At least that's one worry off our mind."

"I guess your parents haven't had any luck raising any money to take him to another hospital," Warren said to Jeff. "Otherwise, we'd have heard from them."

"I know that God is taking care of him," Irene said. "I can't exactly explain it, but ever since I invited Jesus into my heart, I've felt peaceful about Eduardo."

As they were walking up to Mr. Domingo's house, Jeff leaned over to whisper to Warren, "How do you think we should handle this?"

His answer reflected his concern about the situation, too. "We have to be careful about who we trust. We can't afford to make a mistake."

Mindy was the first one in the front door, and let out a scream that brought the others running.

Mr. Domingo stood in the middle of the living room, his face distorted with rage. The two large chairs had been overturned. Foam stuffing had been pulled loose from the underside of the sofa and both chairs. The area rug had been crumpled and pushed against one wall, the sleeping mats carelessly tossed on top of it. What had once been a table lamp was now a pile of broken blue clay pieces lying next to a bent shade. Pillows, magazines, a cracked ashtray, candy, and nuts littered the floor. The only thing undisturbed was the stack of newspapers in the corner.

They were speechless. The others ran to check their personal belongings, and found them in complete disarray. Jeff's suitcase had been turned upside down and all its contents spilled out on the floor. His carefully documented records of the team's expenses were wadded up in a ball.

"What in the world happened, Mr. Domingo?" Warren asked anxiously.

Mr. Domingo turned on him angrily. "You should know what happened! You have something that belongs to someone else. They want it back. They left a note saying they would be back to get it."

Jeff and Warren exchanged worried looks. Jeff knew that wherever Warren had hidden the envelope, it hadn't been found yet.

"Oh, Uncle, I'm so sorry," Rebecca apologized. "We'll clean everything up."

Mr. Domingo's face was livid, and he was trembling all over. His hair was wet and matted, and perspiration was rolling down his face. His dark eyes flashed. His voice boomed through the room. "Forget about the house! They'll do more than wreck my house if you don't give them what they want!"

Mindy's eyes filled with tears. "Let's call Mom and Dad."

"You *should* be frightened, young lady," Mr. Domingo snapped. "The people who did this will stop at nothing to get those pictures."

"How did you know they were looking for pictures?" Jeff asked quickly. As soon as the words were out of his mouth, he could have bitten his tongue.

"So you do have some pictures," Mr. Domingo screamed, ignoring his question.

Warren stepped between the two. "Yes, they found some interesting pictures at the dump. We'll be glad to turn them over to the right person."

"Give them to me. I'll see that the right person gets them," Mr. Domingo offered.

"We might do that," Warren said. "But if we do,

I'd like to go with you to deliver them to the mayor."

"My department works directly with the mayor's office. You don't need to go with me."

"Uncle Fernando, we came here to help your country," Rebecca pleaded. "Why are you acting this way? We need your help now."

"Just give me the pictures," Mr. Domingo ordered.

"And what if we don't?" Warren asked.

Mr. Domingo kept blotting his face. "Then you'll never get home alive. You're dealing with dangerous people, not amateurs. And they won't give up until they get what they want."

"Let us think about it," Warren said. "Right now we're going to take Rebecca to the embassy. When we get back, we'll give you our decision."

Mr. Domingo stomped around the house in frustration. Then he snapped, "Before you go anywhere, clean up this mess."

A few minutes later he slammed the front door and left the house without another word to any of them. They tried to put the place back in order as best they could.

"Tell me the honest truth. Do you think we can trust your uncle?" Jeff asked Rebecca cautiously while he was sweeping up.

"I certainly hope so. He's changed a lot since I last saw him. He seems to be under some kind of pressure. He acts like he's scared, too."

Mindy leaned closer toward Warren. "Do you think they found the pictures?"

Warren smiled. "I doubt it. Or why would they have threatened to return?"

Waiting in line at the embassy was old hat now. It took almost an hour before the group finally made it to the clerk's window.

"We're here to pick up a new passport for Rebecca Estrella," Warren said. "If you remember, her other one was stolen at the airport."

The agent ruffled through a stack of papers. "Sorry. I can't issue that yet. We've been given orders to put a hold on it. There seems to be some concern that you might try to smuggle her out of the country."

Jeff couldn't believe his ears. "Rebecca is an American citizen. We can prove it," he said indignantly. "Let us make a phone call home and you can talk to her principal at our high school."

"Sorry. I have my orders. That's final."

Warren put a hand on Jeff's arm to restrain him, and said, "Let's get out of here."

As they left the embassy, Mindy said, "I don't understand why all these bad things are happening to us!"

"Simple. Now I'm sure we're in a war," Jeff said. "The powers of darkness want to stop us from doing anything for God in Tondo. We have to fight back. We have to become the army God is trying to make us into." Warren nodded in agreement.

"Do you think the passport problem is linked in any way to those pictures?" K.J. asked. "Irene thinks everybody is on the take. Maybe they paid somebody off who works in the embassy."

"Whether there's a connection or not, we're almost forced to ask Mr. Domingo to help us now," Warren said reluctantly. "Unfortunately, he may be our only chance."

Mr. Domingo was sitting in the living room when they got back to his house.

"Have you reached a decision?" he asked as soon as they entered.

"We need your help. We want to have a meeting with the mayor," Warren said.

Mr. Domingo jumped out of his chair and started waving his arms. "What's the point? You're not here to meddle with the politics of our country."

"Well, can you set up a meeting or not?" Jeff asked.

"The mayor's too busy. He wouldn't want to see you."

"Would he want to know that his assistant is involved in organized crime?" Jeff asked.

"That's ridiculous! Where did you get that idea?"

"I have some evidence to back it up."

"Let me tell you something, young man. An hour ago, I received a phone call from a man who claimed to be part of the group who tore up my house. He said his group would see that you would get new airline tickets home and Rebecca would get a new passport if you cooperate with them."

"So somebody *was* paid off!" K.J. exclaimed.

"These people are powerful and dangerous," Mr. Domingo continued. "You don't know who you're dealing with."

"I say we take them up on their offer," K.J. said quickly. "I didn't come here to shake up a whole government."

"Give us a few minutes," Warren insisted. "I want to talk to my team."

"Have it your way, but remember, time is running out," Mr. Domingo warned.

The group gathered in the girls' room to discuss their options. "They kind of have us over a barrel, don't they?" K.J. asked. "Let's give them what they want."

"K.J., we can't be intimidated by their threats. We have to do the right thing no matter what it costs," Jeff said.

"Is getting ourselves killed considered the right thing?"

"I can't understand my uncle," Rebecca interrupted. "He seems to be even more upset than we are. You don't suppose they're paying him off, too, do you?"

K.J. stood up. "Look, I came here to make a video. That's all. Let's quit trying to be the big heroes and save the government. There will always be corrupt government officials."

"I'm surprised at you, K.J.," Mindy cried. "Where's your backbone?"

"Right now I'm just trying to save it."

Warren put his hands up. "Enough of this. We're

wasting time. We have to talk to Jeff and Mindy's parents right away. They've got to have some connections who could help us."

"We'll stall for time until we can talk to them," Jeff said. "Let's tell Mr. Domingo we need one more day." They all agreed and went back into the living room.

"We need another day to think about it," Warren told Mr. Domingo.

Rebecca's uncle jumped to his feet, his lips quivering and his eyebrows meeting in a scowl. "Very well," he shouted. "If that's your decision, I want you and your stuff out of my house in 30 minutes. I'm not risking my life because of your stubbornness.

"Furthermore," he raged, "you've put my niece in real danger. Without a passport, anything could happen to her."

"What do you mean, Uncle?" Rebecca asked.

"You heard about the man who was kidnapped? You might just disappear like he did!"

Chapter 8

Hiding

"Disappear? They wouldn't dare do that to an American citizen," Jeff said.

"I'm sorry, Rebecca," Mr. Domingo said. "Your friends have hard heads. I tried to protect you, but without a passport, it'll be impossible to prove who you are."

"You don't seem to care very much for your niece, do you?" Mindy asked.

"Actually, I do. Getting out of here is the safest thing for all of you. Now hurry up and leave!"

The group packed as quickly as they could. K.J. finished first and went to talk to Mr. Domingo who was sitting on the couch. Jeff wondered why K.J. was being so friendly to the man. He made a mental note to ask him about it later.

Getting a taxi in an emergency didn't prove easy. There were plenty on the streets, but right now they all seemed to be full. The whole team jumped up and down and waved wildly every time one came in sight until finally one stopped.

Rebecca quickly gave the driver instructions to the hospital. Warren had decided to ask Irene to help them find a place for Rebecca to hide out for a few days. She was their biggest concern since she had the added passport problem.

As soon as they entered the hospital, they bumped into Dr. Sanchez again.

"Oh, good. I was hoping to see you today. I've been thinking about some of the things you said," he began, "and I'd like to hear more about what you called 'God's plan.'"

Now Jeff was faced with a big decision. They were in the middle of a crisis. Yet he hated to let an opportunity like that slip away.

"We've got a real emergency going on right now, sir. But I promise to come back and talk to you just as soon as I can."

"Another emergency? Boy, you kids sure like to live on the edge, don't you?

"By the way, you'll be pleased to know that Eduardo is doing better. We still can't find any indication of brain wave activity, but several people have seen him moving different parts of his body. Don't ask me to explain it."

"Irene's family must be thrilled," Mindy said.

Irene came to the door of Eduardo's room. "Did I hear my name?"

Mindy ran to meet her and peeked in the room. "We just heard the good news about Eduardo! God is at work here. And He doesn't begin something that He doesn't plan to finish."

"We're so thrilled. My mother and I have been right by his bedside praying all the time. Day and night."

Jeff asked Irene to come out into the hall, and Warren filled her in on what had been going on.

"We've got to find a place to hide Rebecca right away," Jeff said. "Her life might be in danger."

Irene took a deep breath. "I told you before that I've got friends who live in the squatter area near the dump. It's not the nicest, but it's a great place to hide out for a couple of days."

"We'll take it. We have a taxi waiting outside. Can you come with us?" Warren asked.

"Yes, just let me tell my parents."

While they were waiting for Irene, Jeff came up with another idea.

"Warren, why don't we ask the doctor who to turn the pictures over to. I trust him."

"I wouldn't trust anybody who doesn't already know about them," K.J. muttered. He pulled a comb out of his pocket and began to attack his hair with it.

Warren scowled at K.J. "Quiet, K.J. We haven't

lost faith in everybody. We have to trust someone. I'll go talk to him."

A few minutes later, Irene came running out of the hospital room. "Well, can you stand any more bad news?" she asked.

"What now?" K.J. cried.

"My father just heard a weather report on his radio. A typhoon is on the way."

"Is that so bad?" K.J. asked.

"Our typhoons are like big hurricanes. They usually strike every July. The winds and rain can be fierce. The people at the hospital should be safe, but we need to pray for the people at Smokey Mountain."

"What about where we're going?" K.J. asked.

"That area is on higher ground. You'll probably be okay, but you may get a little wet," Irene said.

"I don't like that word *probably*. This trip is turning into a lot more than I bargained for," K.J. muttered. "And just think. It's only Wednesday."

They took a taxi as close as they could to their destination. When they got out, Irene said, "It's just a few blocks from here. We'll have to carry your luggage and follow the railroad tracks to get there."

"Does a train really run through this place?" Mindy asked.

"Once in a while. Let me take Rebecca in alone first. I'll run into a store and try to get something to disguise her."

She came back with a big, floppy red hat with a brim which fell low enough to shade a great deal of Rebecca's face.

"You guys wait here. I'll be back for you as soon as I can."

Rebecca and Irene took off down the tracks. Irene struggled to help carry Rebecca's luggage, which probably weighed as much as she did. Jeff tried to get a feel for the area while they waited. It seemed to stretch out for miles—one broken-down shack after another. Hundreds of them all lined up. Sometimes he couldn't tell where one stopped and the next one started.

The railroad tracks wound around the rows of shacks. From what Jeff could see, life seemed to be going on pretty much the same as anywhere else: kids tossing and catching balls or playing some kind of made-up games, women scrubbing away at dirty laundry on rusted washboards or rough stones, men working around their houses or gathering in groups to talk.

There were even what appeared to be little "mom and pop" stores scattered around. Signs on the outside of them indicated that they sold everything from rice to candles.

Mindy started laughing. "Look at those kids. They don't have a stitch of clothes on."

Jeff looked where she was pointing at some naked and half-dressed children sloshing themselves and each other with filthy water. A few had T-shirts on, but nothing else.

Then some of the scruffy little kids became aware they were being stared at and ran up to the team.

"Hi, Joe," one of the smallest ones said. He threw

his arms around K.J.'s knees and held on for dear life.

"Here we go again," K.J. said. "My name is K.J."

"Hi, Joe," the others chimed in. K.J. shrugged.

"Hey, wait a minute. There are some kids in uniforms. They must be in summer school," K.J. said. He indicated a group of young boys in blue shorts with white shirts and girls in tailored pale blue dresses standing together. "Doesn't it seem odd to see children dressed so nicely in a community like this?"

"I'll bet their moms go crazy trying to keep them clean," Mindy said.

In a few minutes, Irene returned smiling.

"I'll take you to meet my friends now. I've hidden Rebecca somewhere else, but it's best if you don't know where. If you absolutely need to know, ask my friends and they'll tell you."

They walked along the railroad tracks through the maze of shacks, stopping once at a little store to buy some bottled water. K.J. even tried to buy some ice cream, without luck.

"Boy, what a great place to bring an outreach team," Mindy said. "Just think of the possibilities. We could spend months just telling these kids about Jesus."

Jeff was trying to memorize their route so he could find his way back alone. So far, it was simple. They had just followed the tracks.

Then they stopped in front of a little shack which reminded him of something he had in his back yard when he was younger. He and his friends had pretended it was a fort. Unbelievably, this shack was two stories tall, and it was somebody's home. A man and woman who appeared to be in their late 40s came out to meet them.

"I want you to meet Robert and Gretchen Guerrero, your hosts," said Irene.

The first thing Jeff noticed was that Robert was quite a bit shorter than Gretchen. He resembled her so much that Jeff would have thought they were brother and sister if Irene hadn't told them they were married. They both had thin, stringy brown hair slightly grayed around their faces. They both had small twinkling eyes and wide happy mouths. When they smiled, which was frequently, they revealed teeth badly in need of dental attention. In fact, one of Robert's front teeth was conspicuously absent. His back was stooped from what must have been years of manual labor. Gretchen's hands appeared lined more from work than years.

"I'm glad you got here in time for dinner," Gretchen said. "It will be ready soon." Then she motioned for them to come in. Irene declined an invitation to even go in, saying she had to get right back to the hospital.

"You can put your things over there," Gretchen said, indicating a corner of the room. "That will probably be the safest spot. We have a typhoon on the way, you know."

There was very little furniture in the room they entered: two lumpy, dark brown overstuffed chairs and a short beige sofa whose upholstery pattern was worn to the point of being almost undiscernible; a low wooden table with a badly chipped and peeling veneer top; and three plump, green floor pillows that were shiny from wear and piped with a stiff brown cording. One lone, feeble floor lamp with a yellow shade stood next to the sofa. Wooden-framed pictures of family members and a woven straw basket crammed with magazines and books served as the room's sole decorations. Missing was a rug to soften the floor.

Mindy looked out the front window at the shacks next to theirs. "What's it like here at night?" she asked timidly.

Robert smiled and his missing tooth was even more obvious. "Well, it's home to us. We don't think much about it, but it can be dangerous. A lot of gangs roam the area after dark. In fact, a baby who lives nearby was hit by a stray bullet while she was asleep just two nights ago."

"Is she okay?" Mindy asked.

"The doctors couldn't remove the bullet. But she's still alive. She seems to be doing a little better."

"Should we pray for her?" Mindy asked.

"Sure. In fact, I'll take you over there tonight after dinner. I'm sure the family would be very grateful."

Warren walked over to Jeff and put his arm around Jeff's shoulders. They seemed more like contemporaries than student and teacher. "Well, we sure didn't envision all these complications when we were planning our trip, did we?"

Jeff admitted, "I'm always amazed at the way the Lord works. We wanted to get close to the people. Well, we couldn't get any closer than this, could we?"

"I hope Rebecca's all right," Warren worried. "We had no choice other than to hide her. I hope she understands that."

"Speaking of hiding," Jeff said, "you never did tell me where you hid the pictures."

"I think it's better if you don't know. Don't worry. They're in a safe place."

Jeff let the subject drop. "What did you find out from Dr. Sanchez?"

"I asked him to help me find an honest man high up in the government. At first he laughed. Then he thought about it for awhile and gave me a name."

"Is he sure we can trust him?" Jeff asked.

"He says he's one of the most respected officials in this country. We'll have to take the chance."

"What's his name?" Jeff asked.

Warren pulled a small piece of paper out of his pocket. "I wrote it down here. It's Juan Oresto. He lives in Quezon City, which is about 45 minutes away. I'll leave you with the team in the morning and go try to find him."

"Okay, but what about the typhoon that's supposed to be headed our way?" Jeff asked.

"I almost forgot," Warren admitted.

They looked out the window and saw large, dark cloud formations beginning to take shape in the sky. They were very ominous, unlike anything Jeff had ever seen. They might not be able to forget about it for long.

Chapter 9

Typhoon

"Boy, it's getting dark around here," K.J. complained as he rubbed his eyes.

Mindy whispered to Jeff, "Isn't that fish I smell cooking? Do you think we'll get sick eating this stuff? The guide books said to watch what we eat."

"Mindy, you ask too many questions. If it's cooked, it should be okay," Jeff whispered back. "But be careful of the water. Be sure you drink the bottled water we bought at the store. And wash your hands whenever you get a chance."

"Dinner's ready. Come join us," Gretchen called after a few minutes. She carried big bowls in from the kitchen, placed them on the table in front of the sofa, and took a seat on the sofa.

Robert joined her and Warren and Jeff each chose one of the side chairs. Mindy and K.J., noting how low the table was, quickly pulled up two of the floor pillows and immediately became obsessed with waving flies away from the food. But Jeff was so hungry that he didn't pay them much attention, and Warren was too polite to cause a commotion.

The biggest bowl on the table was filled with rice, and next to it was a plate of fish and another bowl containing a green vegetable.

Mindy volunteered to pray: "Jesus, thank You for these wonderful people who have welcomed us into their home. Thanks for their warm love and this food. Please protect Rebecca from harm, and protect us from the storm that's headed our way. Amen."

After everyone had filled their plates, they ate while Jeff entertained the Guerreros with tales of the club's past adventures.

When they were through eating, Gretchen refused all offers to help clean up, saying that it was not her custom to allow guests to work in her kitchen.

Mindy walked over to the front door and opened it a crack to peek outside. "Wow," she said, "look at those clouds. I've never seen any that dark. A big storm sure is headed our way."

Robert joined her and said, "I can't tell for sure, but I don't think it'll hit for a couple of hours yet."

Jeff and Warren began discussing their plans for shooting the video.

"God obviously had more things in mind for us on this trip than we knew about," Warren said. "But I still believe we'll do the shoot. I'm just not sure how or when. I'll concentrate on getting us some equipment tomorrow so we can do it on Friday."

"That's cutting it awfully close, isn't it, Warren? We're leaving on Monday."

"I don't know if I can go back and leave Rebecca here. I haven't decided yet what to do about that."

Gretchen came back in the room and made a suggestion. "If you would like to, we can go pray for the baby now. I'll take you to their house."

They walked a short distance to an even smaller shack than the one the Guerreros lived in. It was so small, in fact, that they had to duck their heads just to get in the door. In the center of the room, a young woman sat on a stiff chair cuddling a tiny baby. She was slowly rocking back and forth and humming a lullaby. A man hovered over the two of them.

The woman looked up when they entered. "Did you come to help my baby?"

"We can't," Jeff said, "but Jesus can. First, tell us what happened."

"A couple of nights ago, some gang members were fighting outside our home. Someone shot a gun up into the air and when the bullet came down, it went through our ceiling and lodged in the baby's head.

"The doctor said it was too dangerous to remove the bullet, so we should take her home and pray."

"Did the bullet do any damage?" Jeff asked, looking at the motionless child with unfocused eyes.

Gretchen took over when the woman began to cry. "They said she'll suffer some paralysis, but they don't know to what extent yet. A lot of people are praying for the family."

Warren motioned for Jeff to pray for the baby. Jeff understood the need for him to take the lead. One of the main purposes of Reel Kids was to let the kids experience God's power for themselves.

Then Jeff asked everyone to gather around him. "Let's lay hands on the baby," he said.

"Father, You know better than anyone the pain of seeing Your child suffer. We ask that You heal this little girl in Jesus' name."

As they prayed, a blinding flash of light filled the room. Thunder rattled the shack and torrents of rain began to pelt the tin roof over their heads.

"Hurry! Let's get home while we can," Robert cried. "The typhoon is here."

K.J.'s eyes grew bigger and bigger. "Man, I've never heard anything like this before. It sounds like a whole orchestra of nothing but drums."

"Hurry, please hurry," Gretchen urged. "We don't have a minute to waste!"

Jeff quickly handed the baby back to her mother. They raced for the Guerrero's shack, holding hands and leaning into the swirling wind and rain as they ran. It was a struggle to stay erect. Jeff was the last to reach the shack and slammed the door behind him.

"How do we keep the water out?" K.J. asked in vain as it began to trickle in around the windows and door. Robert and Gretchen just shook their heads.

The wind howled louder and louder until it sounded like a pack of wild animals wailing. The shack began to vibrate so much that their dinner table overturned and one leg splintered, falling loose against the floor. Soon K.J. and Mindy were shaking almost as much as the shack. Mindy took refuge in a chair, curled up in a ball with her long legs tucked underneath her, and covered her head with a pillow. Their sleeping mats sailed back and forth across the room from one wall to the other.

Smash! Whack! Smash! Whack! They could hear things crashing against the outside of the house.

"How bad does this get?" K.J. cried desperately.

"Sometimes, homes fly apart during typhoons. There's nothing we can do," Robert said.

"What about this house?" Mindy called out from under the pillow.

"We'll just pray that God will take care of us," Robert said.

The room was so dark now that Jeff could no longer see his hand in front of his face. The roar was so loud and so constant that they could barely hear each other. Water began to seep in through every crack in the walls. Jeff crawled around on his hands and knees in the darkness in search of a dry spot. And still, the storm seemed to be gaining in intensity.

"This is getting bad," Warren cried. "Let's pray."

Each of them cried out to God for mercy.

Suddenly, one section of a wall blew away. Whack! Whack! Whack! They were now being pelted by objects from outside.

"Oh no! Part of the house is missing!" K.J. cried.

"There's nothing we can do," Robert yelled. "Just hold on to something."

Jeff was drenched. He kept saying the same prayer over and over and he could hear other voices praying out loud, too. He was getting more afraid by the minute.

K.J. cried out, "How long do these things last?"

"Sometimes hours. Sometimes days," Gretchen yelled back.

Jeff crawled around on the floor over soggy magazines and shattered pictures until he found the chair Mindy was curled up in. He had passed by Warren and K.J. clutching onto the couch for dear life. Jeff could feel the water rising on the floor and by then he was so scared that he could barely move.

"This is a bad one," Robert said.

"Do you think it'll end soon?" Warren yelled.

"Doesn't look like it," Robert yelled back.

With another loud swoosh, another section of wall ripped away.

Mindy started screaming. Jeff turned his head and faced the full horror of the storm. He blinked against the force of the wind and watched as sheets of water rolled off the roof and crashed onto the ground.

"What do we do if it gets any worse?" he cried.

"It can't get any worse, can it?" K.J. yelled.

"You never know," Robert yelled back. "Just be prepared to make a run for it."

Chapter 10

Kidnapped

Mindy grabbed hold of Jeff's arm. "We're not going to die, are we?"

"We'll be okay," he assured her.

"Then why is half of that wall missing?"

"Just hang on."

The winds howled more fiercely, and Jeff felt the water swirling around his ankles. He was glad Mindy had her legs tucked under her so she couldn't feel the water. For once, K.J. was silent. Jeff thought maybe he had just given up on trying to make himself heard.

Jeff closed his eyes and locked his arms around Mindy's chair in a vise-like grip. He had no way to judge time, but he stayed in this position for what seemed like an eternity. Finally he thought the wind was dying down and the rain stopping. He saw people groping about in search of shelter. He could barely see outside, but it was enough to tell that many of the shacks around them had been completely flattened.

"Do you go through this every year?" K.J. asked unbelievably.

"Many times," Robert answered. "The typhoon season lasts from July to October."

"Why don't you move?" Mindy asked.

"Where would we go? This is home."

When the sun came out and shone on Jeff's face, he was amazed to realize that he had drifted off to sleep sometime in the early morning. He was even more amazed that his teammates were still asleep on top of chairs, sofa, and pillows. Soggy straw mats and magazines floated in the receding water.

They must have slept for hours. Mindy's face looked peaceful, and K.J. was even snoring. Warren was just beginning to stir. Only Robert and Gretchen were missing.

Jeff walked over to where half a wall was left standing, and spotted Robert outside, his stooped back bent over a pile of split boards. He appeared to be sorting them into some kind of predetermined stacks. Gretchen was helping some other women move a heavy table to drier ground. Everyone seemed intent in picking up pieces of what had once been homes and lives.

Warren sat up and blinked his eyes and groaned. "Boy, do I have a headache," he said, running a hand across his short thatch of hair.

"Wasn't that unbelievable?" Jeff asked.

"Like nothing I've ever seen or ever want to see again. Where is everybody?"

"You mean Robert and Gretchen? They're outside helping to clean up."

Warren glanced at his watch. "It's late. I've got to get going and find Mr. Oresto."

"I'll stay here and help," Jeff offered as Warren stood up and smoothed his wet shirt, tucking it inside his equally damp slacks. As he left, he said over his shoulder, "Make sure somebody checks on Rebecca."

Jeff roused a reluctant K.J. and Mindy, and they ventured outside, pushing aside debris and shuffling through trash. Huge sheets of metal roofing lay in heaps amidst broken furniture and broken glass. Personal items were mixed with appliance and furniture parts. The railroad tracks were covered with litter.

"This is too much," K.J. observed. "They might as well just leave things and start over somewhere else."

"They don't seem to feel that way. Why don't we pitch in and see if we can help?" Jeff suggested.

"I'm hungry," K.J. moaned.

"Forget it. So is everyone else."

Gretchen must have heard him or just anticipated their need. "There's some bread and jam over there on that table, and we can make hot tea or coffee."

Mindy stared at her in amazement. "You mean you plan to cook something in the middle of all this?"

She swept her hand across the scene.

"I think you'll be amazed at how fast we get on with our lives," she said, her wide face breaking into a smile. "By tonight, this neighborhood will look as good as new." They all stared at her in disbelief.

"Gretchen, I hate to bother you, but is there any way you can check on Rebecca for us?" Jeff asked.

"I already have. She's okay. She made it through the night better than we did. She's just worried about her passport."

They kept busy with clean-up for hours. Remnants of the storm were quickly gathered, sorted, and heaped in big piles. Mindy and K.J. frequently marveled at how organized the people were. Obviously, they had done this many times before.

They became so engrossed in the process that they were startled when they heard a woman screaming. They turned to see the young mother of the injured baby standing in the center of a crowd.

"My baby is healed! My baby is healed!" she cried, clutching the infant against her breast. Her face beamed as she proclaimed over and over, "My baby is healed. The prayers of the Americans did it."

Jeff dropped the trash he was carrying and ran over to her. He saw that the baby was moving her arms and the blank stare was gone from her eyes.

Some of the people in the crowd began to cry for joy. Then, without warning, Jeff heard the woman urging everyone to go get their sick relatives and friends and bring them to the team for healing.

As lines began to form, Jeff almost fainted when

he saw Rebecca standing at the edge of the crowd. Her bright colored dress made her stand out.

"You shouldn't be here, Rebecca," he said worriedly as he rushed over to her.

"I wouldn't miss this," she said, tossing her long black hair. "And I don't care what they do."

"Well, since you're already here, come and help us pray for these people," Mindy said.

Over Jeff's protests, Rebecca joined the rest of the team. Jeff climbed on top of an overturned box, and Robert stood next to him to translate his words for the people who didn't understand English.

Jeff decided to clear up one thing from the start. "We didn't heal the baby. It was the power of Jesus Christ working through us that healed her."

He felt himself growing bolder. "Some of you already pray every day," he said. "But I want you to know how you can have a personal relationship with Jesus. The first step is to ask Him into your heart."

The crowd quieted as they gave Jeff their attention. Then he volunteered, "We're willing to pray for the sick as long as everyone understands where the credit belongs. Now all those who want prayer, come forward and form four lines."

Jeff motioned for Rebecca, Mindy, and K.J. to each head a line next to him.

The people who had waited so patiently began to come forward one by one. Some of them were weeping; all of them had hope written across their faces. It was hard to imagine that this had been a scene of devastation just a few hours earlier.

When Jeff stopped, it was already 1:30 in the afternoon; they had been praying with the people for hours. Finally the last few left. Only Robert and Gretchen, the mom, and her baby remained.

"I still can't believe the hunger these people have for Jesus," Jeff said to Mindy.

"Speaking of hunger, I think we could all use some lunch now," Gretchen said.

Jeff looked at Rebecca in alarm. "Not Rebecca. We may have pushed our luck too far already." Turning to her he said, "You need to hurry back to where you were. A lot of people must have seen you here." He didn't breathe easily until he watched her walk back up the railroad tracks until she was out of sight.

"My life will never be the same again because of you," Robert said.

"You have blessed us, too," Mindy assured him.

"No, you don't understand. A few minutes ago, I asked Jesus into my heart for the first time," Robert said. His small eyes crinkled with joy. "I've never felt such a sense of peace."

"I feel the same way as Robert," Gretchen added.

While they ate lunch, Jeff, Mindy, and K.J. shared more with them in order to strengthen their new faith. They were instructing them how to study the Bible and pray when a man came running up and interrupted them. He leaned over and whispered something in Robert's ear. The look on Robert's face left no doubt that something was very wrong.

"I'm afraid to ask, but what is it?" Jeff asked.

"Rebecca didn't make it back."

Chapter 11

Threatened

Jeff's stomach began to churn. There must be some mistake. He had just watched Rebecca walking back to safety.

"What makes him think that?" Jeff demanded.

"Some women saw something," Robert said.

"What do you mean 'something'?" Jeff pleaded. "Tell me what you mean by that."

Robert's face fell. "Some women told him that they saw three men pull a struggling girl into a house. She was screaming and fighting them. A few minutes later, the men left the house carrying a very large rice sack, large enough to hold a person."

"Why didn't they try to stop them?" Mindy asked angrily.

"They thought they were part of a gang," Gretchen said. "They were afraid of them."

"Let's not panic yet," Jeff said. "Are you sure the women even know what Rebecca looks like?"

"The girl they described looked exactly like her. They said she had long, dark hair and was wearing a blue and red flowered dress."

"I knew it. She shouldn't have shown up here," K.J. said. "That was dumb."

"It's a little late for that," Jeff snapped at him.

"Well, what do we do now?" Mindy asked.

"Warren will be back soon," Jeff said. "Poor Warren. I almost dread seeing him. Every time he comes back from somewhere, we have more bad news. He's really going to be upset when he hears this. About all we can do now is ask everyone to pray for Rebecca."

Gretchen and Robert joined them in going from house to house to solicit prayer. Jeff knew that if they had ever needed God's help, it was now.

As soon as Warren walked in, Mindy burst into tears. Jeff explained what had happened, and Warren's face turned pale.

"I do have one good piece of news," he said. "I found Mr. Oresto, and he offered to help us. In fact, he gave me his address and wants us to stay at his house."

"How's that going to help Rebecca?" K.J. asked.

Warren ignored the question. "I think we'd better take him up on it."

They quickly gathered their things together and thanked the Guerreros, then raced off with a promise to return as soon as they could.

When they were leaving, Gretchen gripped Jeff's arm with a wrinkled hand. "I feel terrible about this. I feel like it's our fault. We should have been able to protect her better."

The words were barely out of her mouth when a teenaged boy ran up and handed Robert a note, then ran off again. Robert opened the note, read it, then passed it on to Warren. "This is for you."

"Oh, no. Not more bad news!" Mindy cried.

Warren read the note out loud: "If you want to see Rebecca alive, meet us at the first fork in the canal at Smokey Mountain at five o'clock. Bring the pictures with you. Don't tell the police, or you'll regret it."

According to Jeff's watch, it was already 3:30. He turned to Warren. "We'd better get moving. Should we go get the pictures?"

"There's no time. We'll just have to stall them."

"Maybe we should call Mr. Oresto," Jeff said.

"They said not to tell anybody," K.J. protested.

"No, they said not to tell the police."

Warren helped throw their luggage into a taxi and gave the driver instructions to the hospital. "On our way, we can stop and see Irene and Eduardo. I'll try to call Mr. Oresto from there."

They ran into Dr. Sanchez right inside the door of the hospital and got his permission to leave K.J.

guarding all their luggage in the waiting room.

"I'm glad you're here," the doctor said to Jeff. "Do you have time to talk now?" He took off his glasses and stuffed them into his shirt pocket.

Jeff glanced at his watch. He had to make a quick decision. He couldn't keep putting the doctor off. They still had an hour before they had to meet the kidnappers.

He didn't hesitate long. "Sure," he said. "I've got a few minutes."

"That's perfect. I'm not very busy right now."

"I'll go use the phone while you two talk," Warren said and took off down the hall.

The doctor led Jeff to an empty room and pulled a sheet of paper out of his pocket. "I've got a lot of questions for you." He began to ask Jeff everything that was on his heart. As best he could, Jeff answered all the doctor's questions and explained God's plan of salvation to him. Before they left the room, Jeff asked if he could pray, and the doctor agreed.

Then Jeff joined Mindy and Irene in Eduardo's room. "He's getting better every day," Irene told him proudly. "He's moving around more all the time. The doctors can't explain it."

Mindy smiled. "Do you suppose that dumb brain wave machine was broken after all?"

Irene shook her head emphatically, her hair swirling about her face. "No, that's not it. They tried two machines, and both of them registered the same."

Irene was anxious to hear about everything that had happened, and Mindy had just finished filling her in when Warren walked into the room.

"I feel better now," Warren told them. "I talked to Mr. Oresto. He said to go ahead with the meeting. He'll have some of his agents watch us from a safe distance.

"I think K.J. and Mindy should wait here while Jeff and I go meet them."

"That's okay with me," Mindy said. "I've had enough excitement for one trip."

Jeff and Warren walked slowly along the canal until they saw a place where it made a sharp turn.

Two men in short-sleeved white shirts and dark slacks were waiting there, leaning against a shack. As Jeff and Warren approached the men, Warren asked boldly, "Are you by any chance waiting for us?"

The heavier of the two answered. "You're late. We were just going to give you a few more minutes before we left. Your friend will be very glad you showed up. She doesn't seem to like staying with us."

"We insist that you release her immediately," Warren demanded.

Both men laughed. "You're not in a position to insist anything. Now give us the pictures."

"You didn't give us enough time to get them," Warren said. "They're too far away."

The first man hesitated and pulled at his chin. "How much time do you need?"

"Until tomorrow at noon."

He seemed to consider it for a few minutes. Then

he said, "That's your last chance. If we don't get the pictures then, your friend will experience some extreme discomfort."

As they walked away, he tossed over his shoulder to Jeff, "And your sister might be next!"

Chapter 12

The Chase

When Jeff and Warren got back to Eduardo's room, they found something new to worry about.

"Did the men you met have on white shirts and dark slacks?" Mindy asked, running over to Jeff. Her lips quivered and her eyes seemed to fill the frames of her glasses.

"How did you know?"

"They were just here. They walked right past K.J. and came into this room. One of them grabbed Irene's arm so hard that I thought he'd break it. You can see how red it is. He told her that Eduardo may never leave the hospital. He said it all depended on you."

"Boy. They sure get around, don't they?"

Dr. Sanchez came into the room. "Did you ever get in touch with Mr. Oresto? I still think he's someone you can trust."

"We've already talked to him," Warren said. "Thanks for the name. He's going to let us stay at his house. Can you keep an eye on Irene and Eduardo for us until we get back here?"

The doctor assured them that he would. "I still want to talk to you some more about what we were talking about earlier," he told Jeff. "I have just a few more questions. And remind K.J. I need to see him Saturday to check those stitches."

Warren looked at his watch. "We'll have to hurry now. I promised Mr. Oresto we'd be at his house by dark."

Warren flagged down a taxi and gave the driver Mr. Oresto's address in Quezon City. "It should take us about 45 minutes to get to where we're going," Warren said. "Let's talk about what we'll do when we get there."

A few minutes later, Jeff noticed that the driver's eyes kept shifting up to his rear view mirror.

"What's wrong?" Jeff asked.

"I think we're being followed," the driver said. "See that blue Mercedes behind us? Every time I change lanes, so does it."

Mindy cried. "I knew it. We're going to be kidnapped, too!"

"I can't take much more of this," K.J. complained.

"Can you lose them?" Warren asked the driver.

"Maybe. I'll give it a try. Hold on."

The driver jammed the accelerator pedal almost to the floor. The taxi lurched once, then took off as if it had just been given the starting flag on a speedway. "I've got an idea," the driver said after a few minutes of high speed maneuvering. "I'll turn into the next taxi station and switch you into another cab."

"Buddy, you'll earn yourself a nice tip if you can pull this one off," Warren promised.

Jeff looked out the back window. The Mercedes was still behind them. It was weaving all over the road trying to keep up with them.

Faster and faster they went, screeching through impossibly tiny openings between other vehicles. The blue car was hot on their tail. Once it even got close enough for them to see the angry expressions on the faces of its occupants.

"Looks like those guys mean business," Mindy said. "I've never seen such determined faces."

Without warning, their driver whipped the steering wheel to the right and sped into a fenced-in lot. As he went through the gate, he yelled something in Tagalog to the man standing guard. Then he raced toward a building at the rear of the yard.

Jeff looked over his shoulder. The Mercedes was stopped outside the gate. Its occupants had jumped out and were yelling and shaking their fists at the guard.

The taxi screeched to a halt by two other taxis whose drivers were leaning against their cabs talking to each other.

"Get out and jump in the closest one. I'll help with your luggage."

They grabbed their bags and threw them into the trunk of the other taxi, then crowded into the back seat. Their driver shouted instructions to one of the men, who jumped behind the wheel of his cab. As he did, he reached over the seat and roughly shoved Jeff's head down almost to the floor. "All of you, hit the floor until we get out of here."

Warren stuffed a fistful of money into the first cabby's hand before he slammed the door. "We can't thank you enough," he said.

They took off through a back gate. After they had been driving a few minutes, Jeff said to their driver, "I'm worried about your friend. I hope he doesn't get in any trouble. We couldn't have made it without him."

"He'll be fine."

"What if they got his license number?" Mindy asked.

"Don't worry about it. We're used to this sort of thing."

They breathed a sigh of relief when a few minutes later the driver said, "You can get up now. There's no one behind us." He stopped long enough for Warren to join him in the front seat.

Everyone was too exhausted and overwhelmed to talk for a few minutes. Then Warren said to the driver, "I just thought of something. Maybe you'd better let us out about a block away from the address he gave you. I don't want to take any chances that someone could still be following us."

"Good idea," the driver agreed.

When the Quezon City sign appeared, Mindy asked, "Hey, didn't the center of the government used to be here?"

"That's right, Mindy," Warren said. "I'm impressed with your homework. They moved it to Manila years ago."

Mindy grinned. "Yeah. Malacanang Palace. That's the place where Mrs. Marcos kept all her shoes. I'd sure like to see it before we leave here."

"We're getting close," the driver broke in. "I'll let you off over there in front of that store, but you'll have to walk a little ways."

It was much later than they had planned to arrive, but Jeff was glad that the darkness would help cover their tracks. However, Warren was concerned that they were running so late.

"Somebody help Mindy with her suitcase," Warren said as he paid the driver.

"Let her carry her own," K.J. argued sourly. "I've got a bad arm."

"You've also got a bad attitude," Mindy said.

"That's enough, you guys," Warren cautioned. "This is no time to get short-tempered." As they walked down the street, he compared the address on the piece of paper in his hand with the numbers on the houses they passed. Finally, he found the one that he had been looking for. A welcome light was burning over the front door.

The others waited with the luggage at the curb

while Warren went up and knocked on the door. After several knocks, he turned around with a puzzled look on his face.

"This is the right address, but it doesn't look like anyone's home."

"Knock again," Mindy said. "My feet are killing me."

Jeff began to think all kinds of bad thoughts: What if Mr. Oresto had been kidnapped now? Or what if somebody had paid him off? What if this had all been an elaborate set-up for them?

"He did tell us to get here before dark," Warren said with a worried tone in his voice. "It's really dark now. I'm not sure what to do." He walked over to a window and peered inside.

"I'm tired," Mindy cried, walking up to the porch and sinking down on the top step. "I can't go any farther. That typhoon wiped me out."

"I agree. I need some rest," K.J. moaned and joined her. "I'm so tired I don't even remember what day it is."

"Thursday," Jeff informed him. "And that's the reason we can't let down now. We're running out of time. We're supposed to start filming tomorrow, and we don't even have any equipment yet."

They all sat down on the porch and stared blankly at one another, too tired to talk any more. Then Mindy let out a loud gasp.

"Oh, no!" she said. "Don't look now, but there's a blue Mercedes coming down the street."

Chapter 13

Shocking News

How did they find us?" Mindy cried, jumping up as the car pulled to a stop under a street light.

A man got out of the car and walked briskly toward the house. He wore a light blue business suit with well-pressed trousers. A white dress shirt and blue and white striped tie peeked from beneath his coat. He was of medium height and muscular, with the body of an athlete. His softly rounded face featured a neatly clipped mustache over a wide mouth. His eyes were friendly and his greeting was warm.

"I'm Mr. Oresto," he said. "Welcome to my home."

There was a joint sigh of relief. Then the group introduced themselves.

"Does everybody around here have the same kind of car?" K.J. asked.

Mindy explained, "A car just like yours followed us tonight."

"You were followed? By a car like mine? That's interesting. It could have been a government car; they're all alike."

"Then you're saying the men who followed us were government officials?" Mindy asked. "That's a scary thought."

"Wait a minute. Let's not jump to conclusions. Come on in and we'll talk about it," Mr. Oresto said.

He picked up one of the bags and ushered them inside. Jeff was struck by how clean and attractive the room was. His eyes were drawn immediately to a lime and chocolate colored sectional sofa between two nubby, green-tweed armchairs. The furniture was grouped on a green and brown shag rug around a massive, square coffee table with carved rounded legs and a glass top. Three large books with glossy, bright covers and a dark green candle in a low brass candle holder rested on the table.

The far end of the living room served as a dining area, with a long wooden table that matched the one in front of the sofa. Six chairs were evenly spaced around the table. A low-hanging brass ceiling fixture was centered over an artificial arrangement of white flowers and green branches.

Mr. Oresto invited them to sit down. "I'm sorry

you won't get to meet my wife. She's visiting her parents in Baguio City, but I'll do my best to make you comfortable in her absence."

Warren brought Mr. Oresto up to date on the events of the last few hours.

"Have you heard anything about Rebecca?" Jeff asked anxiously.

"Sorry. Nothing yet. We're still trying to identify the men you met by the canal."

Jeff turned to Warren. "I'm really worried about her. She must be frantic by now."

Warren turned back to Mr. Oresto, "What do you think they'll do to her?"

"As long as we have the pictures, I think she's safe. That's what they're after."

"What should we do with the pictures?" Jeff asked.

"You can give them to me in the morning. They are in a safe place, aren't they?"

Before anyone could answer, the phone rang and Mr. Oresto went into another room to answer it. When he came back, he turned to Warren. "Well, there's a new development. That was one of my agents. Your camera bag just showed up."

"You're kidding," K.J. said excitedly. "That's great. Did they find out who took it?"

"Yes, an airport official had it at his home. He's a close friend of Rebecca's uncle."

The words pierced like a knife.

"So, it wasn't taken for its monetary value," Warren said. "Mr. Domingo is involved after all, isn't he?"

"It looks like it—up to his eyebrows. He must have ordered your equipment stolen so you'd have no reason to stay in the country. He had to have been worried about your being in his house with all his underworld connections. Rebecca might have become suspicious of something."

Warren looked worried. "The envelope is still at his house. How will we get it now?"

"You can go there in the morning. I'll think of a ruse to get him out of the house. But I don't want to arrest him until we have Rebecca safely back."

Jeff sank deeper into his chair. The realization was just beginning to hit him. "Even with our equipment back, I don't know if we have time to get everything done."

Mindy shot a sideways glance at Jeff. "Don't even think about it. Rebecca is the only thing important now. I still find it hard to believe that her uncle would be involved in anything that would endanger her."

"This whole trip has been a complete loss," K.J. said. "What are we going to tell everyone when we get back home?"

"How can you say that, K.J.?" Mindy asked. "Are you forgetting all the people who came to the Lord after the typhoon? And don't forget Dr. Sanchez. And Irene and her mother. I'd say we've accomplished quite a lot."

"You're right," K.J. said. "But I still think we shouldn't have gotten involved in all this other stuff."

"It wasn't exactly our idea to get involved in any of it, K.J. And hey, the trip isn't over yet," Jeff reminded him, suddenly taking heart himself. "Loosen up." Then Jeff felt embarrassed. "I'm sorry, Mr. Oresto. We don't always argue like this."

Mr. Oresto smiled. "It's okay. You're under a lot of strain. But at least you can be assured that my men are doing all they can."

"Thank you, sir. We really appreciate it. Rebecca means so much to us," Mindy said.

"Now, tell me more about this water project of yours."

"Let me tell him," Mindy said. "We wanted to do something to help the people who live on the garbage dump in Tondo. We found out that a water system could be put in there for about $5,000. So we decided to come here and make a video to help raise the money."

"How much of that money do you think would have made it to the water system?" Mr. Oresto asked.

"Not much with Mr. Domingo in charge," Jeff admitted.

"If you truly can do what you say you can, I have friends who will make sure every cent goes toward the project," Mr. Oresto offered.

"That's the best news we've had yet!" Jeff said. Then his face fell. "But how are we going to raise the money if we can't make the video?"

"You forgot. We have our equipment back now," K.J. said. "Thank You, Lord."

"He came through again, didn't He?" Mindy said.

Mr Oresto broke into a smile. "Well, I can help

you, too. I know the shortness of time has Jeff worried. I'll make sure you get protection tomorrow so you can make your video as quickly as possible."

"That sounds great," Warren said. "But I still don't know how we can go on without Rebecca."

"I'm sure your friend would want you to finish what you came here to do. That's the best thing you could do for her."

Jeff was thankful for the smell of fresh coffee when he woke up the next morning. He would need a clear head with so much left to do. The fact that it was already Friday weighed heavily on his mind.

He dressed quickly and went to the dining room. Warren and Mr. Oresto were already there at the table, their heads close together in deep conversation. They stopped talking abruptly when he entered the room.

Sweet rolls and a pitcher of juice were waiting on a tray next to the coffee pot. Plates, cups, and napkins were neatly laid out.

"Do you think we could visit the Guerreros?" Mindy asked hopefully when everyone was seated around the table. "They might have remembered something that would help us find Rebecca."

Everyone looked toward Mr. Oresto.

"I don't think you'll be able to. You'll need to keep moving to make your appointment with the men at noon."

"What about our equipment?" Jeff asked.

"It's waiting for you at the airport. You can pick

it up after ten this morning."

"What time can we start filming the video?" K.J. asked.

"I'll have my men meet you at the canal at two," Mr. Oresto said. "That'll give you time to get your equipment and go by Mr. Domingo's house."

"How are we going to get to all these places?" Jeff asked.

"One of my men will be here to pick you up in a few minutes. He'll be driving a blue Mercedes."

"What else?" K.J. laughed. "This is going to be so cool. Our own government car and driver."

Warren waited for the laughter to die down. "Now let me be sure I've got this right. Are we to turn over the envelope to those men?"

"Absolutely not. My agents will be watching everything from a safe distance. Once the contact is made, we'll take over."

"That's fine with me," Warren said. "I've seen too much of those men already."

When Jeff walked into the airport, he remembered how mad he had been at K.J. for letting the camera bag out of his sight in the first place. That single incident had been only the first of all their other problems on this trip.

Mr. Oresto's agent had come with them to speed up the process of reclaiming the lost bag. The agent pointed to a counter in the very back of the waiting area. "They should have it over there," he said.

"I'll need to see some identification," the clerk

said when Warren gave him his name.

The agent stepped forward and flashed his ID card. "It's okay. Mr. Oresto has personally approved this."

"That's good enough for me," the clerk said, and pulled the familiar black bag from under the counter. "But before you leave, check to make sure everything is inside. Then you can sign for it."

"Yep. Everything's here," K.J. said, rummaging through the bag and taking a quick inventory. "Airline tickets, equipment, and..."

"...And Rebecca's passport?" Mindy asked. "Let me look at her picture."

She stared at it for a few minutes and began to cry. Jeff put an arm around her shoulders but was unable to console her.

"We've just got to find her, Jeff," she managed to stammer. "I never got a chance to tell her how much she meant to me. I hope it's not too late."

When they went back outside, Jeff pointed to the name of the airport written above the entrance: Ninoy Aquino International Airport.

"Wasn't Aquino the guy who was shot returning from exile in America?" K.J. asked.

Mindy jumped in with a grin wide enough to bare all her braces. She loved to recite details. "Yes, in 1983. About 26 people were tried for involvement in his murder, but all of them were acquitted. Anyway, his death ultimately led to the fall of Ferdinand and Imelda Marcos.

"Aquino's widow was elected president in 1986, but Marcos refused to acknowledge it. When both of them were sworn into office, millions of people took to the streets in protest. It wasn't until the military and the United States put pressure on him that Marcos withdrew and fled to Hawaii. That's an example of what 'people power' can do."

"How did you know all this?" K.J. asked.

"Research," Mindy said smugly.

"Is Mrs. Aquino still president?"

"No, they have a new president. He's trying to clean up the corruption."

"I wish he'd worked a little harder before we got here."

They all rode comfortably in the air-conditioned Mercedes all the way to Mr. Domingo's house. When they pulled up in front of the house, the agent hit the dashboard with his fist and exhaled a long sigh.

"What's wrong?" Jeff asked.

"There's not supposed to be anyone here, but I see some people walking around inside the house. Wait while I call Mr. Oresto."

Jeff watched while he punched some numbers on the car phone. It was difficult to follow the conversation from what he could hear of it.

Jeff looked at his watch and began to panic. It was already 11:30. There wasn't much time left before they had to make their rendezvous at the canal.

"There's been a change of plans. You can't go in

the house now," the agent said when he put the receiver down. "You'll have to go to your meeting without the envelope and hope for the best."

They still had five minutes to spare when they reached the site of the scheduled meeting, but there was no sign of the men. Something was definitely wrong.

Jeff saw Mr. Oresto approaching them at almost a gallop. His suit jacket was thrown open and his tie was askew.

"Something went wrong, didn't it?" Jeff asked.

"Yes, everything has fallen apart."

"What happened?" Mindy asked.

"They've already got what they wanted."

Chapter 14

Shooting at the Mountain

How could that be? I hid the envelope in the tool shed. I put it inside an old box under some heavy books," Warren said. "There's no way anyone should have been looking for it there."

Mr. Oresto pursed his lips and pulled at his mustache. "I'm really concerned about this. It's bound to have very bad implications for Rebecca. There's no reason for them to let her go now."

K.J. leaned closer to Mr. Oresto and said confidently, "Don't worry. Mr. Domingo would never let them hurt his niece. Trust me."

"What makes you so sure?" Mindy demanded.

It dawned on Jeff that K.J. was the only one of them who hadn't condemned Mr. Domingo. And he also remembered how friendly K.J. had been to Mr. Domingo right before they moved out of his house.

Something funny seemed to strike them all at once and they turned accusing eyes on K.J.

"What makes you so sure, K.J.?" Jeff repeated louder.

K.J. was looking down at the ground, avoiding everyone's stare. He ran his comb through his hair nervously. "Well, at least I trusted him. I'm sorry, you guys. I thought he was on our side. Even after what Mr. Oresto told us last night, I didn't believe Rebecca's uncle would do anything bad."

"What do you mean 'you're sorry'? What are you talking about?" Warren pressed.

"I told Mr. Domingo where the pictures were. I didn't think it would hurt anything if he knew."

Everyone gasped. Jeff almost felt sorry for K.J. when he saw the stricken look on his face—almost, but not quite.

"Just when did you tell him?" Warren demanded.

K.J. hung his head. "At the hospital yesterday. When you guys went to meet those men and Mindy was in with Eduardo and the others. I was watching our luggage in the waiting room. He showed up and we just got to talking."

"Oh, no," Jeff groaned, afraid to hear the rest.

"He said if he could only get the pictures, he might be able to save Rebecca's life. He seemed so upset. So I told him where they were."

"But you didn't know where the pictures were," Warren protested.

"No, but I knew you had to have hidden them somewhere on his property. We never saw them again. I told him that much."

"Well, that explains the people running around his house," Jeff said. "They were still looking for the pictures. They obviously hadn't found them yet when we were there."

"I'm sorry," K.J. whimpered again. "Wouldn't the rest of you have done what I did?" He was answered by their disbelieving stares.

"Mr. Oresto, what do you think will happen now?" Warren asked.

"Nothing would surprise me. They probably figure they can do anything they want with Rebecca now that they have that envelope."

"So where do we go from here?" Jeff asked.

"I'll launch a massive citywide search for her. That's the best we can do."

"What about our video shoot?" Warren asked.

"My agent will stay with you in case there's any trouble. I think you should go ahead with it right now if you're ready."

Warren walked over to K.J., who was openly weeping, and put his arm around him. "Sometimes what we think is best at the time doesn't work out to be that way. Rebecca wouldn't hold it against you, K.J. I'm sure she would be the first to forgive you."

K.J. looked up with guilty eyes. "Maybe she would, but I don't know if I can forgive myself. I've really blown it this time."

Jeff was delighted to have something to do to keep his mind busy. They discussed their strategy while they set up the equipment.

Jeff pulled a piece of paper out of his pocket. "The other day I got an idea about how I think we should do this. Let's get a group of people together and have them explain exactly what the biggest needs are here on Smokey Mountain. We'll make sure they focus on the water problem."

It was even easier than he had imagined to pull a group together. In fact, they were amazed at the co-operation they received. Everyone seemed to know that they were friends of Eduardo's, and they were anxious to ask about his condition. Many of them had also heard about K.J.'s accident, and asked how he was doing.

Warren pulled at Jeff's sleeve and said, "Remember, I'm just here to observe. I want you to take charge of everything."

That was all the go-ahead Jeff needed. He jumped on top of a large truck tire and began waving his arms to attract attention.

"Hi, everybody. Thanks for coming. We've got a special project on our heart. We're here to produce a video to help you raise money for a good water system. Every peso raised will go toward the project.

"The way you can help us is to go about your work like you always do, and let us film you doing it. Then we'll need to interview some people."

"Let's get some good shots of the children first," K.J. suggested.

"That's a great idea," Jeff said encouragingly.

K.J. followed some of the kids around and took pictures of them at play. Then he switched the camera to the adults, capturing them busy at their regular jobs. He made sure to take lots of pictures of people carrying heavy water containers to various sites on the dump.

"Are we ready for those interviews?" Jeff asked.

"I'll strap the mike to a long pole," K.J. said by way of answer.

Jeff looked at his watch while K.J. prepared the mike. It was 4:30, and he was satisfied that the daylight would be okay for a while. Warren and Mindy lined people up to be interviewed, and Mindy stopped from time to time to enter things frantically on her laptop. Her real work would take place after they got back home. It would be her job to write the video script.

Everything was progressing smoothly until they saw Irene running toward them.

"Help! Help!" she cried. "We left Eduardo alone for a few minutes. When I got back to his room, a stranger was standing over his bed. He was disconnecting the life support system!"

Chapter 15

Help from the Palace

"Why would anyone want to hurt Eduardo?" Mindy asked.

"I don't know," Irene cried. "Come quick. We'll try to figure it out later."

"Jeff, you and K.J. will have to finish up alone," Warren called out. "I'll leave Mr. Oresto's man here with you, and Mindy and I will go with Irene."

Dr. Sanchez was holding the door to Eduardo's room open when they got to the hospital.

"What happened?" Warren asked.

The doctor was visibly shaken, his eyes even wearier than usual. He twisted his stethoscope as he spoke. "A man came in here complaining about chest pains. When the nurse went to find me, the man slipped into Eduardo's room and started pulling his tubing out."

"Is Eduardo okay?" Mindy asked.

"Yes. Thank heaven Irene returned when she did. Eduardo will be all right."

"Why in the world would anyone want to hurt him?" Mindy asked again.

The doctor put an arm around her shoulders. "Mindy, in our country, revenge is a very strong motivation. Forgiveness doesn't come easy. Some people are obviously angry at Irene for helping you, and they're taking it out on Eduardo."

"That's not fair. I hope they catch the man who did this and send him to prison for the rest of his life!" Mindy cried.

Warren looked sadly at her, and Mindy realized what his look meant. "I guess I need some lessons in forgiveness myself," she admitted.

Soon Jeff, K.J., and the agent came running into the room, breathing heavily. "We stashed the equipment in the trunk of the car and got here as soon as we could. Is everything okay?"

"For now it is," the doctor said. "But we can't afford to take any more chances. We'll have to make sure someone stays with Eduardo at all times."

"Hey, this might be a good time for you to take a look at K.J.'s stitches since we're already here," Warren suggested. "Then we'll head back to Mr. Oresto's house and see if he has any more news."

"That's a good idea," the doctor agreed. "By the way, Jeff, I read the Scriptures you suggested, and I'd like to tell you a few things I've discovered. About this Jesus...."

Late that night, the team was waiting in the living room when they heard Mr. Oresto's car drive up.

"Have you found Rebecca yet?" Jeff asked, racing for the front door.

"No, but we're closing in on them. My men have a strong lead on their hiding place. We think the man they kidnapped last week is with them, too."

"Where are they?" Mindy wanted to know.

"You wouldn't know the place if I told you. It might be best if you didn't know anyway. Trust me," Mr. Oresto said.

"We do trust you. We'd be helpless without you," Jeff said.

Mr. Oresto smiled. "I do have a bit of good news for a change. I've set up a very important meeting for you tomorrow at Malacanang Palace. The mayor and a special aide to the president will be there."

"You're kidding," K.J. said in disbelief.

"No, I'm absolutely serious. The mayor is very interested in your water project. He wants to help in any way he can."

"Why's that?" Jeff asked.

"He's trying to clean things up here. He's seen a lot of his pet projects blocked with unexplained delays. Obviously, the money allotted to them has been siphoned off elsewhere. It's probably in some bank accounts outside the country by now."

"Isn't that what Marcos did?" Warren asked.

"Yes, I'm afraid so. If we had even half the money some of our leaders have taken from our people, our economy would be in pretty good shape."

Jeff was almost speechless over the news about the meeting with the mayor. He asked, "What time is our appointment tomorrow?"

"You're scheduled to meet at 3:30. I'll have an agent drive you there. In fact, I'll even go with you. I need to check on something at the hospital, but you can pick me up on the way."

"That's perfect," Jeff said. "That'll give us time to visit the area where the Guerreros live in the morning. I've got an idea for another video, and I wanted to do some filming there."

"Look," Mindy cried, as they walked along the railroad tracks the next morning, "there's that little store where Irene bought the hat for Rebecca. I can't believe it's still intact after the typhoon."

Jeff walked between the tracks, fascinated by how much they sparkled in the morning sun. He couldn't believe how peaceful the scene was now. When he considered how quickly the people had put their lives back in order, he was humbled once again by the power of God working through people.

The closer they got to Gretchen and Robert's house, the more bright-eyed children began to follow them and tug at their clothes.

"Looks like we made some pretty good friends here," Warren said. He reached down to scratch the head of one toothy little boy.

Robert and Gretchen greeted them with smiles and hugs, even one for the agent.

Jeff looked around the house and had to admit to his friends, "You were right. You'd never know a typhoon came through here a few days ago.

"We've only got a couple of hours," he said. "We'd like to take some pictures, if you don't mind."

While K.J. began to hurriedly set up the equipment, Jeff explained his idea to the Guerreros. This video would be a simple testimony to the healing power of God. They first wanted to film the young mother with her baby. They would let her tell her story in her own words. Then they would interview some of the people the kids had prayed for, and have them tell what the prayers had meant to them.

Everything went off like clockwork, and they finished in record time.

"We'll have to go now," Jeff said when he saw how late it was. "But maybe this video will inspire some other people to come back here and help you."

They were hurrying so fast that Jeff failed to notice that Mindy had stopped dead still in front of him, so he plowed right into her. He followed her gaze to where three men were standing in the middle of the railroad tracks directly ahead of them. He had never seen two of them, but the man in the middle was Mr. Domingo. He was obviously nervous. His long, dark hair was plastered to his head in fat, messy curls, drops of sweat fell from his face, and his bushy eyebrows met in a straight line.

When Warren tried to go around the men, Mr. Domingo reached out and grabbed him.

"Where do you think you're going?" he asked, shoving Warren to the ground.

"Don't say anything to them," Warren warned the others.

Mr. Domingo leaned over Warren and raised a clenched fist as if to strike him. The agent quietly put his hand on the butt of his gun.

A crowd began to form. Jeff noticed that it included a number of men they had prayed for and interviewed. The crowd grew larger and more vocal by the minute.

"Leave them alone," one of the men in the crowd shouted, stepping forward. Then more people began to yell, and someone climbed on Mr. Domingo's back while others pinned his arms to his sides. The strangers with Mr. Domingo stumbled backward. The agent took his hand off his gun.

"This is none of your business," Mr. Domingo protested loudly, trying to get his arms loose.

"We're making it our business," one of them said. "These are our friends. Turn around and walk out of here now, or you won't be able to walk at all."

The crowd moved away a bit, and Mr. Domingo jumped to his feet and dusted himself off. He seemed unsure what to do next. It had become obvious that he was now alone in his fight.

Finally, he spoke. "Okay. We'll leave." Then,

scowling at Jeff, he said, "But we're not through with you yet." He and his two friends left.

Warren thanked the men from Smokey Mountain for coming to their rescue, and Jeff turned to the agent.

"I wonder what they wanted from us. They've got Rebecca. They've got the envelope. What more could they possibly want?"

By the time they got to the hospital, Mr. Oresto was pacing back and forth outside like a runner eager for a race to begin. He jumped in the car and said, "Let's go. We'll just barely make it."

Jeff's first question to him was, "Have you found Rebecca yet?"

"No, but we're getting closer. It takes time to track down all the leads.

"Let me brief you about our meeting. The mayor is a very respected leader; a man you can trust. His name is Luis Medina."

"Why is the meeting at Malacanang Palace?" Mindy asked. "Isn't that where the president lives?"

"That's right, Mindy. You know a lot about our country. He's out of town right now, but a representative of his will be there."

"Boy! I didn't realize we were that important," K.J. said.

When they came to a large wrought iron gate, Jeff recognized the palace behind it. He had seen pictures of it in a book. He had read that it had been built by a Spanish aristocrat and expected an impressive building, but this place more than met his expectations.

"Wow," Mindy exclaimed, "this would look like a college campus with that beautiful lawn if it weren't all fenced in. So that's where Ferdinand and Imelda Marcos lived."

"For 20 years," Mr. Oresto said. "Twenty long years."

"Was it really that bad?" Jeff asked.

"It's no secret that they stole billions from our citizens. They made even more money from guns, prostitution rings, drug running, and other illegal activities."

Mindy asked playfully, "Did she really leave behind 1,200 pairs of shoes when she fled the country?"

"And a lot of other things, too," Warren kidded.

"Well, I didn't want to mention that," Mindy giggled. "You're probably talking about the five hundred sets of underwear she's supposed to have had."

Mr. Oresto laughed. "Now I'm really impressed with your thoroughness."

Then Mindy became serious. "I wish I could enjoy all this, but I'm so worried about Rebecca. I read that crooks here sometimes take young girls to other countries and sell them as prostitutes. Is that true?"

"Let's not think the worst yet," Mr. Oresto said. "Anyway, it would be hard to get her out of the country with our agents on the lookout for her."

They got out of the car and began walking toward their meeting place. Jeff was impressed with the magnitude and beauty of the grounds, the tall buildings covered with ivy, and the ornate wrought iron fences and gates.

"Over there is where the Marcoses used to live," Mr. Oresto said, indicating a majestic structure. Then he pointed to a smaller building. "Our meeting will be in there. Please follow me."

They were ushered into a reception area filled with vases of long-stemmed fragrant flowers, and they waited until a beautiful young Filipino girl came out and motioned for them to follow her. She led them into a small, red-carpeted room where two finely dressed gentleman were seated.

Mr. Oresto made the introductions.

"I've heard great things about your group," the mayor said. "I'm sorry about all this trouble with your friend."

"Thank you, sir," Jeff said.

"I can assure you that if my assistant, Mr. Laurel, had anything to do with this, he will be brought to swift justice. I've placed him on a leave of absence until the matter is cleared up."

Then the mayor shifted the discussion to the water project. Jeff was amazed at how much both men already knew about it.

"If your video can generate the money you think it can, we'll see to it that every cent you raise goes toward helping the people at Smokey Mountain," the mayor assured them.

"We also have come up with an idea to help your friend," he went on. "We believe in the power of people."

"We do, too," K.J. muttered. "It just saved our skins."

The presidential assistant stood up. "I've taken the liberty of setting up a television interview for your team tomorrow morning."

"Why would you do that, sir?" Jeff asked.

"We want to give you an opportunity to tell our people about your video project. And while you're doing it, you can ask for help in finding Rebecca."

The mayor broke in. "Don't worry. Our people will help you find her."

Warren leaned forward. "We appreciate the offer, but I'll have to call Rebecca's parents first to get their okay."

"We understand. The interview is set for eleven o'clock. Millions of people will be home from work and watching television on a Sunday. Please let us know as soon as possible whether or not we should go ahead with the plans."

The receptionist walked in. "I'm sorry to disturb you, but there's an urgent phone call for Mr. Oresto."

Mr. Oresto got up and left the room while the others continued to talk. When he returned a few minutes later, the worried scowl on his face gave away his concern.

"A girl has just been found who fits Rebecca's description. We're not sure of anything yet, but we need you to make an identification."

Mindy asked guardedly, "Is she alive?"

He took his time answering, and when he did, his words chilled them all.

"Just barely."

Chapter 16

Dead End

"The girl has been badly beaten. In fact, she's unconscious," Mr. Oresto said.

"Well, at least she's alive," K.J. said hopefully.

"We'll go see her right away. We may not need the interview now," Warren told the mayor sadly.

The mayor placed a hand on Warren's shoulder. "I'd still like you to tell about the water project on TV."

"Thank you, sir. We'll call your office to let you know tonight," Warren promised.

"I'll give you my personal number," the mayor said, scratching it out on a piece of paper. "You can reach me anytime tonight."

Jeff remembered to thank the presidential assistant before they left. As soon as they were outside, Mindy's face grew worried. "How long will it take us to get to her?"

Mr. Oresto showed his concern, too. "Barring anything unforeseen, about 20 minutes."

All the way to the hospital, Jeff clung to the hope that Rebecca would be okay. At least their long ordeal was almost over, he thought. They'd fly home tomorrow if Rebecca were in any condition to travel.

They stopped at the counter in the hospital waiting room and asked for directions to the girl's room.

"Room 536. You can take the elevator."

Their anxiety level rose as the elevator stopped on every floor to let people off and on. Jeff could hardly wait to see the girl, yet the closer they got, the sweatier his palms became. He wasn't sure that he was ready for the sight that might be awaiting him.

Mindy ran down the hall and barged right into the room. She walked straight to the bed, leaned over the tiny bandaged figure lying there, and took an agonizingly long look.

Jeff watched as Mindy squeezed her eyes closed and swallowed deeply. Then she slowly opened her eyes and turned to the others. She exhaled slowly.

"It isn't Rebecca."

Mr. Oresto took her arm. "Are you sure? Look again. She's been beaten pretty badly."

"Yes, but I know my friend. This is not Rebecca."

Jeff leaned against the wall and slid down it until he was in a squatting position. He clamped a hand over each ear and dropped his head between his knees. Then he let out a long, relieved sigh. Warren and K.J. just stared at each other in silence.

Mr. Oresto put an arm around Mindy and led her away from the bed. "I'm very sorry to have put you through this. Our men thought for sure they had found her. She was even dressed like Rebecca."

"I can't take any more of this," Jeff said and slowly stood up.

Warren came to his side. "Don't give up now. I don't know where we go now, but we can't give up."

"What do we do?" Mindy cried.

"We do the television interview," K.J. said, brightening. "It's our last hope."

"We'll call the mayor and tell him to go ahead with it," Mr. Oresto said. "I'll take care of the details."

"Thanks," Warren said. "But I still need to call Rebecca's parents and get their permission to show her picture on television."

Before they left, Mindy went back over to the young girl's bed. "We're forgetting something. I think we should pray for this girl while we're here. Remember, she's just as important to God as Rebecca or anyone else is. In fact, I think that God gave us this scare to remind us of that."

"You're right, Mindy," Jeff said. Then the team circled the bed and each member prayed for the girl. Her eyes were still closed, but her face seemed more at peace when they left.

Mr. Oresto unlocked the front door and took Warren into his bedroom to use the phone.

Jeff sank into the couch and stretched his legs out. He was so tired he could hardly hold his head up. Mindy sat down in one of the chairs and took off her glasses. She rubbed her tired eyes with both fists.

"So many good things have happened. I'm really grateful; don't get me wrong. But I still can't understand why Rebecca hasn't shown up."

"I don't know, Mindy," Jeff said weakly. "I just don't know."

K.J. walked over to stand in front of them. "I guess life has its bitter and its sweet. Who would have dreamed we'd be at Malacanang Palace today?"

"Even less likely, who'd have dreamed we'd be on national television in the Philippines?" Jeff agreed. "We'll reach more people that way than with any video we could possibly make."

"Still, with all our good luck, I can't forget about Rebecca," Mindy said defiantly. "If I have to stay here forever to find her, I will."

Warren came back in and said, "I talked to Rebecca's folks. It's okay with them to do the interview and show her picture on television. They're planning to fly over here Monday to help look for her."

"I'll bet they're really upset," Mindy said.

"Of course, but they're still glad Rebecca came on this trip. They know it was the right thing."

"Did you talk to my parents, too?" Jeff asked.

"No. Why don't you try to call them?"

"Yeah. Ask them for some tips for our interview," Mindy said. "They may be my folks, but I still think they're the best in the business."

"Hey, you guys, hold up. I can't keep up with you," Mindy complained as they hurried along the canal the next morning. She glanced at the murky water as they ran along, still searching for its slimy bottom. Since it was a Sunday, only one bulldozer was at work, and the relative quiet was a blessed relief.

"We don't want to keep the TV crew waiting," Jeff said.

"They're not going anywhere," she said.

K.J. was the first to spot them. "Boy, look at those cameras. How would you like to have all that stuff to work with?"

"They must be with a major news network," Mindy said as her eyes grew wider. She shoved a bright blue ribbon up higher on her ponytail and smoothed her blue cotton skirt. She brushed off the shoulders of her matching blouse. "Do I look okay?"

A man in jeans and denim shirt walked over to meet them. He thrust out his hand. "I'm the news director. Sorry about your friend."

"Thanks," Jeff said as he grasped the outstretched hand. "Maybe you can help us get her back."

"We'll sure try. We'll be ready in about twenty minutes. Let's go over the questions I'll ask you."

They had time for a quick rehearsal before the actual interview, which lasted much longer than any of them had imagined. Each member of the team was given an opportunity to talk at length.

When it was finally over, Jeff couldn't contain his excitement. "Do you realize that we were just seen all over the country talking about Jesus? And all this came about because of what happened to Rebecca. I just wish she could have seen it."

"Maybe she's watching," K.J. said hopefully.

"Okay, now. The next thing we need to do is go back to the hospital and check on Eduardo," Jeff said. "And I want to see Dr. Sanchez once more. I don't want to leave him with any questions I could answer."

Irene was waiting outside Eduardo's room. "How is he?" Jeff asked as they went in together.

"Not much change."

Jeff had been certain that their prayers for Eduardo would have been answered by now.

"I'm surprised about that. I dreamed last night he was up and walking around. It seemed so real."

"Please tell me your dream," Irene begged. "I need to hear something good to keep me going. Eduardo moved his arms and legs again this morning. More than ever this time. But I'm waiting for him to open his eyes."

Mindy went over to his bedside and stroked Eduardo's forehead. "I can't believe I love this kid so much, and I hardly know him."

She brushed his hair back and picked up one of his hands. Suddenly, she jumped back.

"He moved his eyes. Didn't anybody else see that?"

The others ran over to the bed. Eduardo's eyes

still appeared tightly closed.

"What do you mean he moved his eyes?" Jeff asked.

"I saw them open and close. I couldn't have imagined it, Jeff. I know I didn't."

Irene began to weep and talk to Eduardo, begging him to open his eyes again. They watched him closely for the next hour, but there was no further movement. Finally, Warren said, "We must get back to Mr. Oresto's house. We have to start packing."

"Goodbye, Irene," Jeff said. "Let us know if there's any change. I still say he'll be all right."

Mr. Oresto held the door open for them.

"I feel terrible about the false alarm yesterday. What a thing to put you all through. I know what that must have done to your hopes."

Jeff said, "Mr. Oresto, your men were just doing their job. That's all anyone can do. Besides, it gave us a chance to pray for that girl, whoever she is. And it reminded us of how important each person is to God."

"Oh, by the way, were you able to identify her?" Warren asked.

"Yes, she lived in the squatter area near your friends, the Guerreros. Her dad was the one who beat her and then left her in a park."

"How is she?" Warren asked.

Mr. Oresto looked down. "I'm sorry. She died."

"Oh, no," Mindy cried. "She couldn't have. She looked so young."

"It happens all too often. I just wish we had some groups like yours here. Maybe we could put an end to some of this senseless pain."

They got up very early on Monday morning. Jeff had hardly slept anyway, realizing that they would have to go home without Rebecca. It would be her parents' job to come here and look for her now.

Mr. Oresto tried to be encouraging at breakfast. "We've gotten great responses from your interview. People everywhere know Rebecca's name and what she looks like now. It's just a matter of time until she shows up."

"I hope so," Jeff said. But he couldn't escape the memory of that young girl lying in the hospital room. He kept imagining Rebecca's face on the girl.

Then the phone rang and Mr. Oresto jumped up to grab it. When he hung up, his face was downcast. He said, "I hoped I could give you some good news before you left, but I'm afraid I can't.

"That was our top agent. We finally discovered the kidnappers' hiding place. They were staying in an old abandoned casino on the west side of town. They found a necklace there with Rebecca's name on it."

"And...?" K.J. demanded.

"...And the room was empty. They've disappeared again. Only this time, we think they might have left the country."

Chapter 17

People Power

What makes you think they left the country?" Mindy asked.

"They found some phony identification papers and passports. If they left those, they probably have others to use to leave the country. It happens a lot."

Jeff started pacing around the room. All he could remember was Mindy talking about crooks taking young girls to other countries and selling them as prostitutes. Surely God wouldn't let that happen!

The phone rang again. "Jeff, it's Irene for you."

Everyone tiptoed over to stand behind Jeff while he talked to Irene.

His face broke into a huge grin. "That's great news. That's great," he kept repeating. When he hung up, he turned to face the others.

"You won't believe it. Eduardo woke up this morning. He even sat up and asked for something to eat. The doctor said he's going to be fine."

Mindy jumped up and down and grabbed K.J. "I knew it!" she said. "I knew all the time he'd be all right. Didn't I tell you?" Then they all joined hands and said a prayer of thanks.

"I'm going to turn the television on," Mr. Oresto said when they had finished. "I'm anxious to see if any other stations picked up Rebecca's story."

He went into his bedroom and in a few minutes, yelled for them to join him. "Hurry! Come quick. You'll want to see this."

Everyone ran into his room and watched as a live news report unfolded on the screen. There were a number of police cars and officers surrounding a van and a group of men. A reporter holding a hand microphone was in the foreground attempting to explain in a loud, excited voice what was going on. Jeff wished desperately that he could understand Tagalog.

"What's going on?" Warren asked.

"Don't you see? They've got them surrounded!" Mr. Oresto said.

"Who's 'them'?" Mindy cried.

"The kidnappers! They caught them just eight miles from here."

"But how do you know? I don't see Rebecca," Mindy said.

All eyes were glued to the screen.

"Tell us what they're saying," Jeff begged.

"They are saying they have Rebecca. She's safe," Mr. Oresto said.

"How can that be?"

"Someone saw your interview and spotted her in a van on the highway to the airport. They must have been planning to leave the country after all. He phoned the police and they intercepted the van. Both Rebecca and the kidnapped man were inside."

"Look," Mindy cried. "There she is! That's Rebecca getting out of that police car right now. I recognize her flowered dress."

"I still don't believe it," Jeff said.

"People power?" Mindy asked.

"How about God's power?" Warren suggested.

"Well, don't forget the power of prayer," K.J. added.

Jeff took one last look at the canal when he got out of the taxi on the way to the airport. It seemed to have fewer insects and fewer oil slicks on it today. He never would have believed that Smokey Mountain could look so good to him. Maybe familiarity had bred an affection for it—or maybe just hope for its future.

"How much time do we have?" he asked Warren.

"Just 15 minutes."

A large crowd had gathered to say goodbye. The Guerreros had come over to see them, too. They could see Gretchen's familiar face over Robert's head. Tears filled Jeff's eyes when he saw Eduardo hobbling toward them, smiling the same toothy grin as the day they had met him. His thin frame was supported by Irene on one side and Dr. Sanchez on the other.

Rebecca was standing next to Mr. Oresto and waving wildly. She had had to give a statement to the police before she could leave the country. Mindy ran and threw her arms around Rebecca and wept for joy. Thankfully, they had been able to get the good news to her parents before they boarded their plane: Rebecca would be coming home with the group after all.

Mr. Oresto said, "Thanks to Warren, those men will spend a long time in jail."

"What's Warren got to do with it?" K.J. asked.

Mr. Oresto smiled. "I guess we can tell you now. Warren and I kept a little secret from the rest of you. The kidnappers did find their envelope at Mr. Domingo's house. They thought they had everything, but Warren had taken the liberty of keeping the letter and the most incriminating picture—the one where the gangster was giving Mr. Laurel the envelope. He's had them on him all this time. We have all the evidence we need. We were just afraid to tip our hand before we got Rebecca and the other man back."

Jeff couldn't decide for a minute whether to be elated or mad. Warren had really pulled one over on them this time. He couldn't be too upset, though. After all, some criminals were going to be brought to justice, and they were going home with their videos.

"Wow! What an ending!" K.J. said.

Jeff broke into a huge grin. "No, I think it's just a beginning."